JEWEL society

battle of
the brightest

by Hope McLean

Scholastic Inc.

For Hana and Ava,
two book-loving sisters who would make
a great addition to any quiz bowl team.

ISBN 978-0-545-60765-0

12 11 10 9 8 7 6 5 4 3 2 1   13 14 15 16 17 18/0

Printed in the U.S.A.   40
This edition first printing, December 2013
Previously published as *Jewel Thieves: Battle of the Brightest*
Book design by Natalie C. Sousa

Chapter One

"This is a crime against fashion!" Lili Higashida shrieked, strapping on a thick black vest.

"It's not supposed to be fashionable," countered her friend Erin Fischer.

"Are you sure this doesn't hurt?" asked Jasmine Johnson, nervously looking around the equipment room, where dozens of laser guns hung from the wall. "I mean, I know it's just lasers, but it looks pretty dangerous."

"Well, once I tripped over my shoelace and skinned my knee," Erin admitted. "But that's about as dangerous as it gets. Actually, this is a miracle of modern technology. See?" Erin pointed to her vest. "The lights on the shoulders show what color team you're on. These ports on your back and chest will register when someone makes a hit. The lights will go off for ten seconds, and when they're on again you know it's okay to shoot."

Lili sighed. "Why couldn't you have chosen something normal, Erin?"

Willow Albern came to Erin's defense. "Lili, this whole 'friendship checkup' thing was your idea, anyway," she pointed out. "And when it was your turn to choose the activity we went to the art exhibit."

"Yeah, well, that was awesome!" Lili said.

Willow rolled her eyes. "It was just a bunch of squiggles. My little brothers can do better than that."

Lili frowned. "Anyway, we wouldn't have to do these friendship checkups if you and Jasmine would just play nice."

Jasmine and Willow looked uncomfortable. Even though they'd been friends since they were little, they had recently been arguing with each other a lot. Jasmine had become so upset that she briefly quit the Jewels, the middle school quiz bowl team the girls competed on together.

"We *are* playing nice," Jasmine insisted. "So don't you think a game of laser tag defeats the whole purpose of that?"

"No, because the purpose of this is fun," Erin said cheerfully.

It was Friday night, and the Laser Emporium in the Hallytown Mall was filling up fast with other players. One mom had brought three young kids into the equipment room, and five teenage boys were suiting up, too.

Another boy wearing a red Laser Emporium T-shirt entered the room.

"Hi, my name is Chip," he said in a bored voice. "I need to tell you the rules now, so pay attention."

Chip explained how the vests worked, just like Erin had. Then he outlined the rules of the game.

"You get fifty points every time you hit someone in the back of the vest, a hundred points if you hit the front," he said. "The targets in each base are worth three hundred points each. There are also hidden targets on the course for bonus points."

"Where are they?" one of the little kids asked.

"I said they're *hidden*," Chip explained, rolling his eyes. "Does anyone else have questions?"

"I do, but I'm afraid to ask," Jasmine whispered to Willow.

"Don't worry," Willow whispered back. "There are lots of places to hide on the course."

"Oh yeah, the most important thing is no running," Chip added. "Now please proceed to the red door."

The teenage boys rushed to the red starting gate, practically knocking over the girls. Jasmine nervously wiped her palms on her leggings.

"How about I just watch?" she asked.

Willow grabbed her hand. "Just lie low, and you'll be fine."

Chip opened the door to a black cavernous room decorated to look like the surface of a strange planet. Large fluorescent orange rocks dotted the landscape, and the walls were painted to show a purple-pink sky with three moons floating in it. Special black lights lit up the space, so the rocks and the sky glowed in the dark. When the girls walked onto the course, it was hard to focus on anything except the colored lights on their own vests.

"The game will begin in fifteen seconds," Chip instructed. One of the teenage boys started to speed away, but Chip stopped him with a booming command. "NO RUNNING!"

Then a robotic voice started to count down over the speakers. "Fifteen . . . fourteen . . . thirteen . . ."

The little kids started trotting away, with their mom hurrying to keep up. The teenagers weren't running, exactly, but they, too, were moving pretty fast.

"Oh my gosh. What do we do? Where do we go?" Lili fretted.

"Stick with me," Erin said. "I got your back."

Erin took off after the teenage boys, with Lili following nervously behind her. Jasmine wanted to stick with Willow, her super-athletic friend, but she, too, was already racing across the course.

Panicked, Jasmine found the biggest rock in the farthest corner and hid behind it.

"Three . . . two . . . one . . . commence play!"

The teen boys all went after one another, darting among the rocks and shooting blast after blast. Erin and Willow snuck up on all of them, scoring points by shooting quickly and then zipping away.

Distracted by her conquests, Erin forgot her promise to watch over Lili, who was soon surrounded by the three younger kids.

Pew! Pew! Pew! They barraged Lili with shots, and the lights on her vest went dead. She shrieked with laughter, despite herself.

"Aaaaaah! They got me! They got me!"

Behind the rock, Jasmine held her breath, hoping nobody would notice her. From the corner of her eye she saw a round red light on a rock hanging down from the ceiling.

Remembering what Chip had said about targets, she took aim and fired at the light. It flashed and then died out.

"Woo hoo!" Jasmine yelled, and then covered her mouth with her hand, but it was too late. One of the older boys heard and walked up to her, shooting her in the back. But Jasmine didn't mind so much. She used her ten seconds to look for another hiding place — and another target.

It seemed like the battle had just begun when the robot voice came over the speakers again.

"Game ending in ten . . . nine . . . eight . . ."

Everyone except Jasmine was zipping around the field like crazy, walking as fast as they could without actually running. Willow and Erin were chasing each other now, laughing. Lili hid, waiting until the three little kids walked past, and then she jumped out.

Pew! Pew! Pew! She hit all three.

"Revenge!" she cried happily, raising her fist in the air.

Jasmine carefully made her way around the perimeter, hitting every target she could find. Then the count was over, and Chip entered the course.

"Okay! Everybody out!"

After they took off their vests and turned in their laser guns, they went up to the front counter, where each player got a printed sheet showing their score.

"Yes!" Erin cried. "I hit that one guy twelve times."

Then she frowned and turned to Willow. "You hit me eight times? Seriously?"

Willow shrugged. "It's all about the points!"

"My score is pathetic," Lili said. "But I have to admit, it was fun."

"I got eleven hundred points," Jasmine said. "Is that good?"

Erin and Willow both stared at Jasmine.

"Are you serious?" Erin asked. "That's awesome! How did you get all those points?"

Jasmine shrugged. "I just aimed at the targets, that's all."

Erin shook her head. "It's always the quiet ones, isn't it?"

"Why? What score did you get?" Jasmine asked.

"Never mind!" Erin and Willow said together, and then they laughed.

Lili put her hands on her hips. "Come on, guys. Friendship night isn't supposed to be competitive."

"Is anyone else hungry?" Erin asked, quickly changing the subject.

"I could go for some pizza," Jasmine answered.

They made their way across the mall to their favorite pizza place, Mario's. It wasn't part of the food court, but a little restaurant all on its own.

"One large plain and four waters?" Willow asked her friends.

Erin checked the pockets of her jeans. "Four bucks each, right? Got it." She handed Willow the cash. "Lili and I will find a table for us."

A few minutes later they were seated at one of the metal tables, biting into slices of hot pizza.

"Sooo good," Erin said, taking in a mouthful at the same time.

Lili giggled. "Erin, you've got cheese all over your chin."

Erin reached for the napkin holder, but it was empty. Willow noticed and flagged down the bus boy, who came back a minute later with a holder stuffed with new napkins. The girls each took one.

"Well, that was fun," Lili said. "It's nice to take a break from quiz bowl practice once in a while, isn't it?"

Jasmine nodded. "Although we need to keep up with practices. We've got Nationals in a few weeks. I can't believe we qualified!"

Willow nodded. "Especially since this is the first year that Martha Washington School has had a team in ages."

"Well, anyway, we still need to practice," Jasmine said. "I bet the Rivals are training right now."

"I bet they practice in their sleep!" Erin joked.

"Except when they're busy stealing jewels," Lili added.

The Rivals, the academic team from Atkinson Preparatory School, were the stars of the middle school quiz bowl scene. They also happened to be jewel thieves.

Willow groaned. "Don't remind me. They're probably plotting how to steal the sapphire at this very moment, if they don't have it already."

"That's what bugs me," Erin said. "For all we know, they could have all four jewels by now, and have already figured out the clues."

The four friends had gotten involved with the Rivals' jewel thefts when the Martha Washington ruby was stolen, and Jasmine was the main suspect. Then they discovered a letter written by Martha Washington herself that said there were *four* special jewels: a ruby, a diamond, an emerald, and a sapphire. According to what the girls had learned, each jewel held a clue etched on the back that led to some kind of important thing — a treasure, maybe. At least, that's what they hoped.

The Jewels couldn't get the ruby back from the Rivals, but they did prevent them from stealing the diamond — for a while. Unfortunately, the Rivals stole it back. And then they went after the emerald, which was owned by a wealthy socialite and TV star named Derrica Girard. Jasmine had held it in her hands, but only for a few seconds. It was with the Rivals now.

"Don't forget what Derrica said," Jasmine reminded them. "She's heard that Arthur Atkinson has been asking around about a sapphire. So I don't think they have it yet."

Arthur Atkinson, the director of Atkinson Preparatory School, had been helping the Rivals steal jewels all along.

"Then we can find it first," Willow said.

Erin nodded. "We tracked down the diamond all on our own. I bet we could find the sapphire."

Jasmine frowned. "Principal Frederickson is watching our every move these days," she said. "She doesn't want us looking for the jewels, and I certainly don't want to get in trouble with her."

"She doesn't have to find out," Erin said, smiling, her mouth ringed with tomato sauce.

Jasmine shook her head. "Napkin, Erin!"

Erin reached for a napkin, but when she held it up to her face she stopped. She wasn't holding a napkin at all. It was a piece of lined yellow paper, folded into a square.

"No way!" Erin cried. "It's another secret message!"

Chapter Two

The girls sat in silence for a second as they gazed at the yellow notebook paper, their eyes wide. It wasn't the first time they had seen a note like this. The same kind of paper had been used by a mysterious helper who had left them clues to help find the diamond.

Erin eagerly began to unfold the paper, but Willow put a finger to her lips and raised an eyebrow. Her gaze scanned the room, looking for whoever could have planted the note. The other Jewels joined in, checking out the room. But nothing — and no one — seemed suspicious. When the busboy walked by, Willow stopped him.

"Excuse me," she asked. "Where do you get the napkins to refill the dispensers?"

He wiped his hands on his apron as he shrugged. "From the big cardboard boxes in the closet. They're not anything fancy."

"Any idea how this could have gotten mixed in with them?" Erin asked, holding up the paper.

The boy sighed as he brushed his shaggy brown hair out of his eyes.

"If you've got a complaint, you gotta tell the manager." He shuffled away quickly before they could ask him anything else, clearly not wanting to get into any trouble.

Lili glanced at her phone. "My mom will be here any second to pick us up," she said. "Let's bring the note back to my house and we'll analyze it there."

After getting a ride to Lili's house from Mrs. Higashida, the girls rushed upstairs to Lili's bedroom. Erin felt like the note was burning a hole in her pocket — she couldn't wait to open and read it!

Lili's bed was piled with sketchbooks, pieces of fabric, plastic gems, and other items from her craft kit.

"So sorry!" Lili hurriedly grabbed a handful of stuff and shoved it into her closet. Jasmine and Willow sat on the bed, and Erin flopped onto the fluffy rug on the floor, clutching the note in her hand.

"Read!" Jasmine cried eagerly, her eyes shining.

Erin unfolded the paper and theatrically cleared her throat. Lili giggled as she sat down next to Erin on the rug.

"Come on," Willow pleaded impatiently.

Erin read the note out loud: " 'We shall meet when the value of seven cubed plus the number of times per month the moon orbits the Earth, adding the year the ceiling of the Sistine Chapel was completed, divided by the number of James Madison. Subtract two. Next add one hundred. Then find me in the place that tinkers are dying to get into but never leave.' "

"Huh?" Lili asked with a frown.

"It's a riddle," Jasmine said. She pulled out a mini notebook from her bag and a small purple pen. "We need to figure it out."

Willow reached off the bed and grabbed the note from Erin's hand. "Hey — help yourself, why don't you!" Erin cried.

"Sorry." Willow grinned sheepishly. "Do you mind?"

Erin rolled her eyes. "Fine, have at it."

"We just had a friendship checkup!" Lili yelled. "Everyone behave."

"Or else Lili will make us use finger-paints and sock puppets to get in touch with our inner feelings," Erin said with a grin.

Lili's eyes got big. "Hey, that gives me an idea!" Willow groaned.

"Guys, enough! Let's focus," Jasmine said sharply as she clicked the tip of her pen. "Willow, read it again slowly."

Willow began. " 'We shall meet when the value of seven cubed —' " She shut her eyes as she ran the calculations in her head. "Let's see, that's seven to the third power or . . . three hundred and forty-three!" she said confidently in the same tone of voice she used when answering a quiz bowl question.

"Okay, so far we have three forty-three," Jasmine said as she jotted the number in her notebook. "What's next?"

Willow continued. "'Plus the number of times per month the moon orbits the Earth.'"

Jasmine snorted. "Simple. If this is a riddle, it's a really easy one. The answer is one," she said as she wrote it down.

"So right now we have three forty-four," Lili said. "What's next?"

"'Adding the year the ceiling of the Sistine Chapel was completed,'" Willow read.

Lili's eyes glowed. "Michelangelo, what a genius! Did you know that it's a myth he painted the ceiling of the Sistine Chapel while lying on his back? He was so super-smart, he invented this totally innovative scaffolding system instead. There are more than three hundred painted figures on that ceiling!" Lili gazed into the distance with a dreamy look in her eyes.

"Um, Lili?" Erin nudged her friend gently. "That's really great and all, but do you know when he finished painting it?"

Lili shook her head as her eyes drifted back to her friends. "Oh yeah!" she giggled. "Sorry. 1512."

Jasmine wrote in her notebook. "That makes the total 1856." She frowned. "How can we meet someone in 1856?"

"Last time I checked I don't own a time machine!" Erin said. "But, man, how awesome would that be?!"

Willow got that stern look on her face, the one she always made when the conversation began to drift off topic. "We're not finished," she said seriously before continuing to read. " 'Divided by the number of James Madison.' "

Lili looked confused. "James Madison is a person, not a number."

"Ha! He is a person who will always be known by one number, and that's the number four," Erin said triumphantly. "Madison was the fourth president of the United States. Whether you look him up in an encyclopedia or online, that's the first thing you'll find out about him."

The others nodded their heads. "Let's keep going and see what we come up with," Lili suggested. "We can always go back and try again if the final answer doesn't make any sense."

Jasmine quickly scribbled. "So that brings us to four hundred sixty-four."

Willow scanned the yellow note. "So next we subtract two."

"Four sixty-two." Jasmine shook her head. "If we add one hundred, that makes five sixty-two. Okay, it's still not making much sense."

"The next part says, 'Then find me in the place that tinkers are dying to get into but never leave,' " Willow read. "This next part of the clue tells us *where* to meet. The first part is *when*."

"Let's focus on the *when* now," Jasmine said. "We have the number five hundred and sixty-two. It can't be a time, and it doesn't look like military time, either."

Lili was thinking hard as her gaze wandered aimlessly around her room. Her eyes landed on the calendar hanging from her wall. Suddenly, she jumped up and grabbed it.

"I think I'm on to something," she said excitedly to the others. "Look," she said as she pointed at today's date. "Today is April thirtieth. Can I see your notebook, Jasmine?" Jasmine nodded and handed the pen and book to Lili. "Written out, the date looks like this." She wrote *4/30* in the notebook and held it up.

"So five-six-two could be a date — like May sixth?" Erin suggested. "But what does the two mean? It can't be the year."

Willow stood up, her eyes shining. "No, but it could be the time."

"Yes!" Erin snapped her fingers. "May sixth at two o'clock. That's next Saturday!"

Willow rubbed her chin with her hand. "But is it p.m. or a.m.?"

"No way am I meeting a stranger at two a.m.," Jasmine said fiercely.

Willow agreed. "That's so not safe. Let's assume that it's two in the afternoon. Now, let's try to figure out where. 'Find me in the place that tinkers are dying to get into but never leave,'" she read.

"Elan's Couture!" Lili cried, naming a fancy boutique the girls had once visited. Everyone looked at her strangely.

"Not the time to be thinking of fashion, Lili," Willow said.

"No!" Lili shook her head, her shiny black hair swinging around her face. "Elan's Couture is on Tinker Street!"

Tinker Street was located in the historic section of River Park, a nearby town.

"That's right!" Jasmine said. "But what near there would be a place that tinkers are dying to get into but never leave?"

Erin gasped. "I got it!" she said triumphantly. "It's the Tinker Street Historical Cemetery. It's really old. I've gone there to do research before."

Lili opened her laptop and began to type. "It says the hours are eight a.m. to five p.m."

"Then the note *must* mean two p.m.," Willow said.

"That's good." Lili shivered. "There is no way I'm going to a cemetery in the middle of the night. In fact, even the thought of going in broad daylight creeps me out a little bit."

"Don't worry, Lili." Erin put an arm around her friend. "It's a busy place. There are a lot of tourists hanging around. They even do walking tours with guides dressed in period costumes. It's not spooky at all."

Jasmine finished writing. "So to sum up, we believe the Riddler is asking us to meet him or her at the Tinker Street Historical Cemetery at two p.m. next Saturday, May sixth."

They all nodded in agreement.

"I find something else interesting about this note," Jasmine said. "It's like each part of the riddle was designed for one of us."

On their quiz bowl team, each member had an area of expertise. Erin handled the history questions, Jasmine took the science section, Willow buzzed in on the math problems, and Lili managed the arts and literature topics.

"Maybe it's all an elaborate plan by Ms. Keatley to get us to study for quiz bowl," Erin joked. Ms. Keatley was the Jewels' quiz bowl advisor and a history teacher at Martha Washington School.

"Whoever sent this note knows us pretty well," Jasmine said thoughtfully. "I can't wait to find out who it is!"

That next Saturday, the girls all piled into Mrs. Higashida's car.

"Tinker Street again?" she chuckled as she shook her head. "You girls do have expensive tastes." The exclusive shops located on the street were known to be a bit on the pricey side.

"Window shopping is totally free!" Erin said, but Jasmine sighed. She loved to look at the glittering gems on display in the jewelry shop windows. She dreamed about owning her own rare gem collection one day.

"But we'll spend most of our time touring the old cemetery this afternoon," Lili added.

Mrs. Higashida pulled into the parking garage. As they left the car, she reminded them to stay together, before heading off to meet a friend on Tinker Street for lunch.

The girls traveled down the cobblestone sidewalk, passing pretty, old brick buildings as they walked. They wore hoodies and sweaters as it was still a bit cool in late spring, but the shining sun high in the bright blue sky was warming everything up.

"It's one forty-five." Willow glanced at her phone. "I want us to be a few minutes early."

"We're almost there," Erin said. "It's right at the end of the block on the left."

The block ended and the girls found themselves standing in front of a tall black gate, which was attached to a black picket fence that encircled the area. Although it was a sunny day, the numerous trees growing throughout the cemetery blocked out the sunlight, filling it with a spooky shade of gray. Old, crooked tombstones jutted out from the ground. The girls spotted several angel statues here and there, some weeping.

Lili shivered. "Maybe we're making a mistake," she whispered.

Erin grabbed her hand. "Don't be nervous."

A woman dressed in a Revolutionary-era costume smiled at them. "Would you like a tour? The next one starts at two."

"No, thank you," Willow answered. "But do you have a map?"

"Yes, of course! Here you go," she said as she handed one to Willow, who took out a dollar from her bag and placed it in the Plexiglas donation box.

"Thank you. Enjoy!" The woman smiled at them as they walked into the old graveyard. "But watch your step. There are some fallen tombstones and tree roots that are easy to trip over."

The darkness seemed to swallow them up as they stepped inside and began strolling down the main path. Erin eagerly began reading the tombstones they passed. Some of the really old ones had skulls and crossbones etched into them.

"Very gothic," Jasmine remarked.

"If you like gothic, then check this out." Erin started to read from a tombstone dated 1789. "'All you that doth my grave pass by, as you are now, so once was I, as I am now, so you must be, prepare for death and follow me.'"

Lili let out a moan. "What time is it? I need to get out of here!"

Jasmine shook her head. "Creepy. But I wonder where we should meet our mystery person?"

The woman who had greeted them at the gate passed by with the two o'clock tour. She was talking about a skull carving on one of the headstones as a group of about ten people followed behind her. The girls scanned each one, but nobody looked familiar or suspicious.

"Let's just stay around here. It's central to the rest of the cemetery," Willow said as she consulted the map, "and we can see anyone who comes in the gate here."

The girls passed the time by reading the tombstones. "'Here lies Mary, the beloved wife of James Selman. She did much good in her life,'" Erin read.

Lili sniffed. "Awww. I should come back and bring flowers for her."

Several people passed through the gate, but they didn't pay any attention to the Jewels.

"It's after two," Willow said. "I wonder if we got the riddle wrong after all."

Erin gasped. "Rats!" she said in a loud whisper. "Of course *he* would have to show up and ruin everything." She jerked her head toward the gate, gesturing for the other girls to look.

Ryan Atkinson, the captain of the Rivals' quiz bowl team, was walking into the cemetery. A tall boy with wavy blond hair, he wore jeans and a blue shirt.

"He might scare away whoever is trying to contact us," Jasmine whispered back.

"Should we try to hide?" Lili asked, panicked.

"It's too late," Willow replied as Ryan began walking toward them. He looked directly at the Jewels and waved, giving them the smug smile they had all come to hate.

"Don't give anything away," Willow whispered to the others as Ryan strode over to them.

Willow looked Ryan right in the eyes. "Hi, Ryan," she said. "Here for the tour? You're a little late."

Ryan grinned. "I'm not here for the tour — I'm here for you. I'm the one who sent you that note, and all the others before it," he said, as the girls went silent in complete shock. "And I need you to help me steal the Atkinson sapphire."

Chapter Three

The girls were totally stunned for a moment. Erin spoke up first.

"What do you mean, *you* sent us the note?"

"It doesn't make any sense," Jasmine blurted out. "I mean, those notes in New York warned us that you were going to steal the diamond. Why would you do that to yourself?"

"We can't talk here," Ryan replied, looking around. "Why don't you follow me to Café X?"

Without waiting for an answer, he turned and began to walk out of the cemetery.

"We should follow him," Willow said. "We need to figure out what's going on."

"Are you serious?" Erin asked, folding her arms in front of her. "I am not going anywhere with that thief. He's probably leading us into a trap."

"Erin's right," Jasmine said, frowning. "We can't trust him."

"It's a public place in the middle of the day," Willow pointed out. "What can he possibly do? Aren't you curious to know what all this is about?"

Lili anxiously bit her lower lip. "I definitely am. I think we should go."

Jasmine sighed. "Me, too, I guess."

"No way," Erin said.

"If anything looks weird, we'll leave right away," Willow assured her.

Erin's eyes narrowed, and she made a low growling noise. "I am going under protest," she informed her friends.

Ryan had already left the cemetery, but they knew where Café X was. The hip coffee shop was on a corner along Tinker Street, with wide windows on the front and side. Several patrons sat at small round tables by the windows and sipped their drinks, watching people walk by.

The girls stepped inside. Ryan was beckoning to them from the back of the room. Seated with him at the rectangular table were the other three members of the Rivals' quiz bowl team: Aaron Santiago, Veronica Manasas, and Isabel Baudin.

Erin quickly turned and started to walk away. Willow grabbed her by the arm.

"Erin, where are you going?" she asked.

"Isabel's here," Erin said. "I said I would leave if I saw anything weird, remember?"

"Very funny," Willow said. "Come on, I'm even more curious now."

The girls sat down, four Jewels facing four Rivals.

"I'm glad you came," Ryan said. "I guess you probably want me to explain."

"Um, yeah!" Erin answered, annoyed.

Isabel rolled her eyes. "I told you it is ridiculous to trust them," she said in her French accent. "This is a big mistake."

"It's ridiculous to trust *us*?" Erin asked incredulously. "You guys are the jewel thieves."

Veronica turned to Isabel. "Just let him do it," she said, sounding even more annoyed than Erin. "I'm sick of this whole thing."

"Will you guys let Ryan talk, please?" Aaron interrupted.

Erin, Veronica, and Isabel got quiet.

"Okay," Ryan said. "It's like this. You know about the Atkinson sapphire, right?"

Jasmine nodded. "It belonged to your school, but then it was stolen, like, seventy years ago."

"Right," Ryan said. "So my uncle Arthur came to us one day and told us that he knew how to get it back. He said we had to find three jewels: a ruby, a diamond, and an emerald. He said that each jewel had a clue on it, and if we got all three, they would lead us to the sapphire."

"Three clues?" Willow asked. "But there are four clues, and they all lead to some kind of treasure, not the *sapphire*."

"I know," Ryan interrupted her. "You see, that's the story my uncle told us at first, and we believed him. We wanted to get the sapphire back, to restore the honor of our school."

"I just wanted to have fun," Isabel piped up.

Veronica shook her head. "Fun? Really? Because I've been miserable this whole time."

"Well, it has been kind of fun," Aaron admitted. "And I mean, we didn't think we were doing anything wrong. We really thought we were going to get the sapphire back."

"Exactly," Ryan said. "But then we started to get suspicious. Lili, remember when we bugged your pen?"

"How could I forget?" Lili asked. "That was really mean!"

"I guess it was," Ryan admitted with a sigh. "So, we were listening to you guys through the hidden microphone in your pen and we heard you talking about four clues, not three. We asked my uncle about it, and he convinced us you guys were wrong."

"That was easy to believe," Isabel remarked, and Erin glared at her.

Ryan continued his story. "But once we got the emerald, my uncle confessed that he had been lying the entire time. He admitted that the sapphire had a clue, too, and once he had all four clues, they would lead to something big."

"Did he say what it was?" Jasmine asked.

Ryan shook his head. "No. But anyway, we realized he had been using us. He said he was close to finding the sapphire and didn't need our help anymore."

"Can you imagine that?" Isabel fumed. "He just tossed us aside, like we were peasants."

"So that's why we want you to help us find the sapphire," Ryan said. "We want to find it before my uncle does."

"But why do you need our help?" Willow asked. "And why were you sending us clues to help us find the diamond? Weren't you trying to steal it for your uncle?"

"Yes," Ryan admitted. "And we had some ideas about where the diamond was in New York, but we weren't sure. So Isabel had this idea that maybe you could help us figure it out."

"Which we did," Erin said, glaring at Isabel.

"I still don't get it," Willow said. "Weren't you worried that we would get to the diamond before you?"

Ryan looked sheepish. "Honestly, we didn't think you had it in you to actually steal it," he said. "Which, technically, you didn't. You out-smarted us after *we* stole it and got it back."

"Just for a little while," Isabel interjected. "Stealing it back from you was like taking candy from a baby, as you say."

"That's because we're not lousy jewel thieves," Erin said hotly. "What you guys did was wrong."

"And now we want to make it right," Ryan said quickly. "Besides, don't you want to get your ruby back?"

The four Jewels looked at one another. This whole thing had started when the Rivals stole the Martha Washington ruby, and the girls wanted it back more than anything.

Jasmine looked suspicious. "How could we get it back if your uncle has it?"

"Once we get the sapphire and find the treasure, we can use it as leverage," Ryan said confidently. "He wants that sapphire pretty badly. He'll have to meet our demands."

"Besides, he already has the clue from the ruby," Isabel added. "That's all he really needed from it, anyway."

Willow was still full of questions. "How do you know the four jewels lead to a treasure? We've been wondering about that ourselves."

Ryan frowned. "My uncle wouldn't tell me," he said, and Willow could tell this upset him. "Uncle Arthur was always my favorite when I was a kid. It felt good to help him — made me feel important, you know? But in the end it was like he didn't care about me at all, unless I could help him."

"But we imagine that the jewels lead to something very valuable," Isabel added. "Otherwise, why would he go to all this trouble to get it?"

"Well, Martha Washington said the jewels led to something important," Erin said. "That's a fact, not a *guess*." She looked at Isabel as she emphasized that last word.

Willow nodded thoughtfully. Everything was adding up.

"So will you help us or not?" Ryan asked.

"We need to talk it over by ourselves," Jasmine said quickly. "Come on."

The four Jewels went to a table in the far corner of the café.

"So what should we do?" Lili asked.

"It's an interesting proposal," Willow admitted. "I like the idea of getting the ruby back."

"And I really like the idea of getting back at Arthur Atkinson," Jasmine said, remembering the embarrassment he had caused her.

"I can't believe you guys!" Erin said. "It is completely ridiculous to think about trusting these losers for one second. They're thieves! You heard Ryan. He used us once to find the diamond. How do we know he's not using us again now?"

Willow nodded. "I get it."

"But somehow I think Ryan is telling the truth," Jasmine added. "I can just . . . feel it."

"I think we should help them," Lili said. "I mean, I really want to know what the four jewels all lead to. And even if the Rivals are tricking us, we might be able to find out."

"I agree," Willow said. "I say let's trust them."

"And I say no way!" Erin said, shaking her head in anger. Then she stormed out of the café.

Chapter Four

Erin furiously stomped out onto the sidewalk and flopped onto a black wrought-iron bench along the street. *Have my friends all lost their minds?* she wondered. *Do they seriously want us to work with the Rivals?* As she shook her head, she felt a hand gingerly touch her on the shoulder.

"Lili," she began as she whirled around, expecting to see her friend. "There is no way I'm working with those jerks and that's that!"

But it wasn't Lili. It was Veronica! She smiled sheepishly at Erin.

"Oh," Erin said. Out of all of the Rivals, she actually liked Veronica and felt a little guilty about what she had just said. "Um, sorry, Veronica. But I don't know how we can trust you guys after everything that has happened."

Veronica let out a huge sigh and sat down next to Erin on the bench.

"I don't blame you one bit," she said, and Erin looked at her in surprise.

"I never, ever wanted to be involved in those jewel thefts," Veronica admitted. "School is really important to me. I'm proud to be on the quiz bowl team. If I could be on a team that won Nationals, I knew it would look really great on my college applications later on." Veronica frowned. "But then Ryan talked us into stealing the ruby. And then the diamond. And then the emerald. Instead of practicing for quiz bowl, we spent most of our time planning the next heist. But I was afraid to say anything. I thought they might kick me off the quiz bowl team, so I went along with it. Quiz bowl is one thing that actually makes my parents proud of me."

A memory clicked in Erin's head. "That's right! Your older sister was Miss Hallytown."

"Yes, my perfect beauty-queen sister, Amelia," Veronica said with a rueful laugh. "And I remember you have a perfect older sister, too."

Erin wrinkled her nose. "Oh, yes, the wonderful and amazing Mary Ellen."

They laughed together.

"But seriously," Veronica said, "Ryan is trying to turn things around. He is really mad at his uncle. And I feel guilty about those stolen jewels. I just want to see them returned to their rightful owners. And I know in order to do it we'll need your help."

Erin let out a deep breath. "I don't know," she said, pausing to think about it. "Hey, I really like your shirt."

Veronica had her long black hair pulled into a messy ponytail. She wore jeans and a T-shirt that had a picture of a petri dish on it that said, "When life gives you mold, make penicillin."

Veronica laughed. "Thanks. You should have seen the argument I had with my mom over it. She always wants me to wear frilly, girly stuff like Amelia does. And she's always giving me my sister's hand-me-downs."

"Veronica, I think your mom and my mom could be best friends." Erin smiled briefly before her face turned serious. "If you pinky swear to me right now that everything Ryan said is true, I will help you find the sapphire."

Veronica held up her little finger. "Pinky swear," she said solemnly. Erin linked pinkies with her and shook.

Erin stood up and then groaned. "I just remembered Isabel. How do you deal with her?"

Veronica grinned and pulled her earbuds out of her pocket. "I wear these a lot when she is talking."

They were both laughing as they walked back into Café X. The Jewels looked up at them in surprise. Erin sat down next to them as Veronica made her way back to the Rivals' table.

"So?" Lili asked hopefully.

"I'm in," Erin said. "But I say we need to be careful. I like Veronica, but I don't trust the others."

"Agreed." Willow nodded. "We'll do this, but we'll be smart. Let's go tell them."

The girls walked back to the Rivals' table and sat down.

"We will help you find the sapphire," Willow said.

"Great!" Ryan replied. "Now let's get started. First, we'll head over to Aaron's house and set up a command center. Next, we'll —"

"Whoa!" Willow put her hand in the air. "Slow down. We said we'll help, but as equal partners." She looked at her friends. "I think we'd all be more comfortable meeting at my house," she said as Erin, Jasmine, and Lili nodded their heads in agreement.

Ryan gave his signature smug smile. "But Aaron has a superfast Wi-Fi connection and a fifty-six-inch television in his bedroom so we can hook up our laptops. I'm sure you don't have those things."

"Whatever we used before, it was good enough to find the diamond for you," Willow reminded him as her eyes flashed. "It's my house or the deal is off."

"Fine," Ryan said reluctantly. "Let's head over."

As they all got up and gathered their things, Jasmine hung back to talk to Willow.

"How weird is this going to be?" Jasmine wondered. "Hanging out with the Rivals at your house?"

"I never would have seen this coming!" Willow said. "But I'm interested to see how they work together. Ryan sure is bossy."

Jasmine worked hard to keep a straight face. Willow could be a bit bossy herself at times!

Back at Willow's house, they all crammed into Willow's small but neat bedroom. The Jewels sat on the bed, while Ryan took a seat at Willow's desk and Aaron and Veronica sat on the floor.

"How quaint," Isabel sniffed as she settled into a beanbag chair.

Erin's face got red but just as she opened her mouth, Ryan took charge.

"Aaron, search for any sapphires that were sold in 1949," he barked. Aaron nodded and pulled out his laptop from his bag. "Veronica, check for any sapphires that may have been donated to a museum around that time." Veronica grabbed her smartphone for the search. "Isabel, continue cross-referencing historical events with sapphires." Isabel took her laptop out and got started right away.

The Jewels watched with their mouths open. "It's like watching soldiers," Lili whispered to Erin.

Ryan turned to the girls on the bed. "As for you, I thought maybe you could —"

Once again, Willow interrupted him.

"Ryan, sorry, but this is not how we work." She shook her head. "And if you're asking us for help, it means you haven't been getting anywhere on your own. I think you should try it our way."

Aaron stopped typing and looked up from his screen. "She's got a point, Ryan. All this research has gotten us nowhere."

"Fine," Ryan said as his mouth tightened. "And what exactly is *your* way?"

Lili jumped in, smiling sweetly. "Basically, we just talk!"

Ryan raised an eyebrow. "How advanced," he smirked.

Willow shot him an angry look as Jasmine spoke. "We brainstorm together," Jasmine explained. She pulled her notebook and pen out of her bag. "Let's start at the beginning. What do we know about the sapphire?"

"It was stolen from Atkinson in 1949," Isabel explained.

Jasmine began to write. "Any idea who stole it?"

Isabel shook her head. "No. There was a police investigation but no one was arrested. In fact, the police were baffled at the time. There were no leads."

"My relatives tried for years to find it," Ryan added. "To their knowledge, it has never surfaced anywhere. It's like it disappeared."

Aaron scrunched up his face as he concentrated. "I did find an old newspaper article from that year that mentioned the Memento Mori," he remembered.

"What's a Memento Mori?" Erin wondered.

"It's a super-secret club at Atkinson that still exists today," Ryan clarified. "It's only for upperclassmen, and no one knows who exactly is a member of the Memento Mori. It's very exclusive, and they're known for pulling outrageous practical jokes."

Isabel laughed. "Everyone suspects it was them who turned the swimming pool green this past St. Patrick's Day."

"Were the Memento Mori around in 1949?" Lili asked.

Aaron nodded. "According to the newspaper article, yes."

The Jewels exchanged glances. "So maybe the Memento Mori stole the sapphire as a joke!" Jasmine guessed.

"But wouldn't they have returned it?" Veronica said. "They're known for playing jokes, not stealing things."

Willow thought it over. "Since we don't have any other leads right now, it's worth looking into," she said.

Ryan shrugged. "It's impossible to get information on them. They're a highly secretive group. Even I don't have any connections to help us there."

Lili smiled. "Not a problem, Ryan. Because I think I do!"

Chapter Five

Eli gripped his flashlight tightly as he made his way through the northernmost section of the Atkinson campus, a remote spot past the sports fields. He had never been back this far, and it felt a little strange. The path he walked on, used mostly by the cross-country team, led directly into a heavily wooded area. It was a few minutes before seven thirty at night but already pretty dark out. He let out a big sigh. *Why do I let my little sister talk me into these crazy stunts?*

Over a week ago, his sister, Lili, had asked him for a favor. "Please, Eli," she begged. "We need to learn more about the Memento Mori. Rumor has it that it's a secret club only for Atkinson upperclassmen. And you're an Atkinson upperclassman!"

Eli knew all about the Jewels; the Rivals; and the ruby, diamond, emerald, and sapphire. In fact, he had helped out the Jewels many times before. He had even planted a GPS device on Ryan once. And now the Jewels were working with the Rivals! He shook his head, thinking how crazy it all was. But he had to admit, he was curious about the sapphire's location and what clue the gem might hold.

So Eli began casually dropping hints around Atkinson that he was interested in joining the Memento Mori. "I heard a rumor that the Memento Mori were responsible for turning the swimming pool green," he said loudly to his friend Zane in the crowded locker room one day after gym. "That was so cool."

He mentioned it to other friends at lunch where he was sure to be overheard. Even getting noticed by the Memento Mori was a long shot, so he was totally psyched when he discovered a mysterious note in his locker the day before:

Ithuotes   Ftesw7nt   Yomtn3ow   Ojmoi0ro

Uommgito   Wieohnhd   Anerttws   Nttrahe

But Eli couldn't make heads or tails of it. He brought it home to show Lili, who was in her room doing homework with Erin.

"I know how to read HTML, but this has me baffled," he told them. "It's letters and a few numbers, but they don't make any sense."

"I love cracking codes." Erin rubbed her hands together. "Codes were used throughout history all the time, to relay orders to soldiers in battle, to exchange messages about secret organizations. You name it, they did it all. Let me at it!"

"Hmmm." She frowned as she studied the note carefully. "It could be a code-word cipher, but I don't think it is. The words are too long. Plus we would have to guess the code word. That could take forever."

She turned to a fresh page in her notebook and rewrote the note out. "Okay," she said. "It's eight words and sixty-three letters total." She grew excited. "I think it's a simple block cipher!"

Erin drew a grid in her notebook, one with eight rows and eight columns. She began to write the letters from the note into the rows. She wrote the first letter or number of each word, and then she went back to the beginning and wrote down the second letter or number of each word. She kept going until all of the letters were in the grid. When she was finished, she sat back and threw her pencil down triumphantly.

"Easy!" she announced. Lili and Eli peered at her notebook.

I	F	Y	O	U	W	A	N
T	T	O	J	O	I	N	T
H	E	M	M	M	E	E	T
U	S	T	O	M	O	R	R
O	W	N	I	G	H	T	A
T	7	3	0	I	N	T	H
E	N	O	R	T	H	W	E
S	T	W	O	O	D	S	

Lili read it out loud: "'If you want to join the MM, meet us tomorrow night at seven thirty in the northwest woods.' Wow, Erin, I'm impressed. That was super-smart!"

Eli nodded in agreement as Erin blushed. "It was nothing," she said modestly.

Lili turned to Eli. "Do you know what they mean by the northwest woods?"

"I think so," Eli said. He brought up the Atkinson website on his laptop and clicked on the campus map.

"Your school sure is fancy," Erin said as she looked at the large drawing that showed six different buildings, as well as sports fields and tennis courts.

"It's big, too," Eli said. He pointed at the screen. "I'm pretty sure they are talking about this part. It's the wooded area behind the sports fields."

Lili looked worried. "Are you sure it's safe?"

"Don't worry, I'll bring a flashlight with me." Eli tried to reassure his sister, but inside he felt a little nervous, too. After all, he didn't know who the members of the Memento Mori were.

After his Computer Club meeting the next day, Eli said good night to his friends, grabbed the flashlight he had brought from home, and made his way through the dark Atkinson grounds. He started on the path that went through the woods and looped to the west.

"I hope I'm right," he mumbled to himself as the woods closed around him. He shivered nervously and ran his hand through his spiky black hair. It sure was creepy back here.

The path started to veer to the left. *I'm almost there*, he thought. The beam of the flashlight created sinister-looking shadows as he walked. He tensed and stood still as he heard a rustling noise in the woods. The sound faded, and he began to travel the path again. His nerves were starting to get the better of him. The flashlight was shaking in his hands. For just a second, the beam of light moved off the path, plunging the trail ahead of him into darkness.

Eli almost screamed when a creature jumped out of the shadows. But it wasn't a creature at all. His hands were shaking so hard that he almost dropped the flashlight. Eli was looking right into the dark hollow eyes of a grinning skeleton!

Chapter Six

Eli's feet were glued to the ground, even though his brain was yelling at him to run. He forced himself to direct the flashlight beam onto the thing in front of him.

Not one, but two skeletons stood before him, blocking his path. *Wait a minute — they're wearing hoodies, jeans, and sneakers!* Eli thought. *They're guys wearing skull masks!* He took a deep breath.

The taller of the two extended his hand toward Eli. In it was an envelope.

"Take this," he said in a deep, muffled voice. "If you accept this challenge and are successful, you will be a Memento Mori. If you fail, you will never hear from us again."

They both nodded ceremoniously at Eli before disappearing into the shadows.

Eli felt his heart pounding in his chest as he hurriedly made his way back down the path, clutching the envelope and the flashlight.

There was no way he was opening it until he was somewhere indoors with lots of light!

The next day, the Jewels called an emergency meeting with the Rivals to discuss what was in the envelope. This time, they all gathered in Lili's bedroom.

"Is it okay to talk in front of him?" Ryan jerked a thumb at Eli.

Lili smiled. "Eli knows everything, and thanks to him we've got a lead on the Memento Mori."

Ryan arched an eyebrow. "Really?"

Eli nodded. "But I'm going to need your help," he said to Ryan. He told them all about his walk through the woods and his encounter with two members of the Memento Mori.

"What's in the envelope?" Erin asked eagerly.

Eli groaned. "It's a task I have to perform. If I can pull it off, I'll be a member. If I can't, it's game over."

"It can't be that bad," Veronica said, but the look on Eli's face made her ask, "or is it?"

"You tell me," Eli said. "I have to steal a pair of Arthur Atkinson's monogrammed boxer shorts and run them up the flagpole for the entire school to see. And I have to do it before this week is over or I've failed. Oh, and I can't get caught, either."

Aaron laughed. "Yeah, dude, that's bad."

Isabel wrinkled her nose, while Jasmine and Willow shook their heads. "How are you going to do it?" Jasmine asked.

"I'm hoping Ryan can help me," Eli said, "although the note was very specific that I had to do it by myself. If they spot anyone helping me, they'll consider it a failure. But I have no idea how to get a pair of Arthur Atkinson's boxer shorts!"

Ryan grinned. "Actually, it's not as hard as you might think. My uncle comes to school early every morning to do laps in the school pool. He brings his gym bag in the locker room. And I'm pretty sure he doesn't wear his boxers while he's swimming."

Eli thought it over. "How early does he get there? I have to retrieve the shorts and run them up the flagpole before anyone else gets to the school. The flagpole is right in front of the main building. I can't have anyone see me doing it."

"He's there by five thirty a.m. So if you grab the shorts right after he gets into the pool, you should have plenty of time," Ryan said. "Only one custodian is there that early. He opens up the buildings. You'll have to time it so he doesn't see you."

Eli groaned again. "I guess I'll be getting up really early tomorrow!"

The next morning, Eli dragged himself out of bed while it was still dark out. He had asked his mom to drop him off. Mrs. Higashida worked in Washington, DC, as a translator and left the house early each day to beat the morning rush hour.

"The Computer Club is lucky to have someone as dedicated as you," his mom said as she dropped him off in front of the school.

Eli gave her a sleepy smile as he got out of the car. His cover for being at school so early was that he was working on the supercomputer, a big project that had been the focus of the Computer Club for the entire year. It wasn't a lie, really. He planned to do just that as soon as he successfully completed the stunt.

Eli climbed the steps of the main building and strode into the deserted school. He walked down the empty hallways and past Arthur Atkinson's office. The lights were on, but the director of Atkinson Prep was not inside, so Eli made his way to the other side of the building, which housed the locker rooms, gymnasium, and indoor pool.

He stopped outside the locker room and listened for sounds of anyone moving around inside. All was silent. Eli slowly opened the door and peeked in. The room looked empty. He noticed a suit dangling from a hanger in front of a locker. On the floor below it was a sapphire-blue duffel bag with the initials "AA" on it. Eli crept quietly toward the bag. A sudden splash from the pool area startled him, but he relaxed once he realized it must be Atkinson diving in.

Quickly, he unzipped the duffel bag and saw a pair of plaid boxer shorts sitting on top. The Memento Mori were right. Atkinson did indeed have his initials monogrammed on them! Eli pulled a pair of scissors out of his backpack. He made two holes in the waistband of the boxers so he could attach them to the flagpole. When he was finished, he stuffed the boxers into his backpack.

With the first part of his task completed, he rapidly made his way through the school back toward the main entrance. The lights in all the hallways were on, but he didn't spot anyone, not even the early-morning custodian.

A glance at his watch told him it was five forty a.m. School wouldn't start for almost two hours, but he still had to hurry before more staff members began to arrive. He raced through the main entrance and approached the flagpole. He quickly untied the rope and lowered the flag to the ground. After removing the flag, he carefully folded it and placed it in his backpack so he could leave it safely in a storage room somewhere when he was finished. He grabbed the boxers and attached them to the rope, then hastily raised the boxers up the flagpole. It was a breezy morning and they fluttered in the wind. He had to laugh to himself. It *was* a funny sight, and the "AA" on the shorts was big enough to leave no doubt about who owned them.

Just then, the door to the main entrance opened. Eli jumped behind a bush and looked up. It was the custodian. Eli watched the man's gaze go to the flagpole. *Oh no!* Eli thought. *What if he finds me here? Will he take the boxers down before the Memento Mori can see it?* His heart pounded in his chest as he tried to be as quiet as possible. Then he heard the man chuckle softly and walk back inside.

Eli let out a huge sigh. He had done it!

Later that day, the entire school was buzzing about the practical joke.

"That was too funny." Eli's friend Zane laughed at lunch. "Everyone on my bus was cracking up when we pulled up to school. I wish I knew who did it. I heard Atkinson went ballistic when he found out."

Ryan walked by his table and winked. Eli wanted to tell his friend Zane the truth, but he knew he couldn't.

By the end of the day, Eli couldn't stop yawning. He was beat from getting up so early. He groggily walked toward his locker and opened it. An envelope fell out onto the floor. Eli quickly scooped it up. The envelope had a red wax seal on it with the initials "MM." Had he succeeded? Was he now a member of the Memento Mori?

Chapter Seven

"Great job, Eli!" Lili squealed, giving her brother a big hug. "I knew I could count on you!"

The Jewels, the Rivals, and Eli had once again gathered in Lili's bedroom. Eli's envelope did indeed contain an invitation to join the Memento Mori.

"I'm in!" Eli beamed. "And I am invited to a meeting next week."

Jasmine laughed. "I wish I could have seen Atkinson's face when he realized his boxers were flapping on the flagpole!"

Ryan smiled. "I did. He was not happy."

Eli grew nervous. "I hope he never finds out it was me!"

Erin crossed her arms in front of her. "If everyone here keeps their mouth shut, no one will ever know you had anything to do with it." She glared at Isabel.

"I know how to keep a secret." Isabel pouted. "But you have a very big mouth, so maybe you should be worried about yourself."

Erin's face grew bright red. "You — you —" she stuttered.

Willow let out a piercing whistle. "Quiet!" she yelled. Isabel and Erin stopped and stared at her, their mouths hanging open. "No time for fighting. Eli has more news to share."

Eli nodded. "That's right. In addition to the envelope in my locker, the Memento Mori emailed me a secret file about the history of their group. I have twenty-four hours to study the file before a code embedded in it causes it to destroy itself. They are going to test me at the next meeting before I am formally initiated." He began typing on his laptop to pull up the file. "Here it is!" he said triumphantly.

They all gathered around the laptop excitedly. Isabel bumped into Erin. Erin turned to glare at her, but a warning look from Willow silenced them both.

Ryan bent his head over the screen and let out a low whistle. "Wow," he said. "It looks like this lists the name of every single person who was ever a member of the Memento Mori."

"Oh my gosh!" Veronica cried as she pointed at the screen. "Erika Douglas, 1985. That's my biology teacher. Her name is Douglas-Kollet now, but she went to Atkinson!"

Aaron pushed his way to the front. "I wonder if any of my teachers are on here," he said.

Ryan cleared his throat. "Excuse me, but we don't have time for this. We only have twenty-four hours before the file is deleted. Let's get to work."

Willow nodded her head. "Agreed," she said. Ryan looked at her in surprise. She shrugged. "When you're right, you're right," she told him with a grin.

Eli began to read from the file. "It has a history of the Memento Mori, too. This is interesting. Memento Mori means 'remember your mortality' in Latin. The group believes in living every day like it is their last, and celebrating life." He smiled. "I'm kind of glad you guys talked me into this. It sounds like it's a fun group to be a part of." His smile turned to an evil grin. "And I might even get used to those skull masks."

Lili rolled her eyes. "Oh no! We've created a monster!"

"I did it all for you, sis," Eli teased back. He returned his attention to the computer and continued scanning the file. "Ryan's right. It has a list of every person to ever belong to the Memento Mori since it first was formed, dated by year."

"Search 1949," Erin and Isabel said at the exact same time. They looked at each other in surprise, while the rest of the group burst out laughing.

"I guess you guys have some things in common after all," Jasmine said. Erin and Isabel rolled their eyes at this comment simultaneously, causing everyone to erupt in fresh peals of laughter.

Eli ignored the ruckus as he typed in "1949." A list of eight names popped up.

Isabel scanned the list. "They must all be old men by now. Some of them might not even be alive."

Willow read the names. " 'Henry Porter. Robert Everette. Thomas Roderick. Lawrence Andover. Walter Donahue. David Wimmer. James Kirk. Arthur Clifford.' I guess we could do an Internet search on each of them and see what we turn up."

Erin tapped a finger to her cheek, deep in thought. "One of those names sounds so familiar, but I can't place it. Willow, can you read them again?"

Willow repeated the list, while Erin shut her eyes tightly. "I know I've heard one of those names recently. It's floating around my brain. I just can't grab it!"

"Think of something completely different," Lili suggested. "That always works for me. Did you see last night's episode of *East Coast Class*? I loved the white dress Derrica wore to the party. Too bad Rhianna threw that glass of punch on her."

Erin got a huge grin on her face. "Lili, I love you!" She grabbed her surprised friend in a hug. "That's it! Derrica mentioned Lawrence Andover on her Chatter page."

East Coast Class was a reality television show about rich socialites in the DC area. The Jewels had had a chance to meet one of the stars of the show, Derrica, when they tried to stop the Rivals from stealing her emerald. Derrica knew all about Arthur Atkinson's involvement with the theft and about how he was searching for the sapphire, too.

Eli handed his laptop over to Erin. She logged into her Chatter account and went straight to Derrica's page, then read one of her status updates out loud: "Congrats to Chad Andover and Amanda Highfield on their engagement. Looking forward to the party this Saturday night at Lawrence Andover's house!"

"Maybe Chad is Lawrence's grandson?" Aaron suggested.

"I know one way we can find out!" Erin began to type. "I'll ask Derrica."

The next day, the Rivals, the Jewels, and Eli sat at Café X again, this time to meet Derrica. She had confirmed that Lawrence was indeed her friend Chad's grandfather, and was thrilled to hear from Erin. She wanted to talk in person as soon as possible.

Veronica looked uneasy. "Is everything okay?" Erin asked as she sipped on a vanilla frappe.

"We stole her emerald," Veronica said. "I feel really bad about it."

Ryan, Aaron, and even Isabel had guilty looks on their faces.

"Derrica is really nice," Jasmine tried to reassure them. "She'll be happy you're trying to help get it back."

Just then, Derrica breezed through the door, wearing oversized sunglasses and carrying a clearly expensive handbag. She let out a little yelp of excitement when she spotted the Jewels.

"Girls!" She hurried over, her high heels clicking on the floor. "It's been ages." She bent to give them all air kisses, then removed her sunglasses and turned her gaze to the Rivals. "Are these the little masterminds who stole my lucky emerald?"

The Rivals all looked uncomfortable, but Ryan spoke first. "We did, and we're sorry," he said while the others nodded. "Once we turned the jewels over to my uncle, he locked them in the safe in his house. But we're going to do everything we can to get it back for you."

Derrica waved a perfectly manicured hand in the air. "I understand. It was all that awful Arthur Atkinson's fault. Water under the bridge. If you can get my emerald back, all will be forgiven." She looked at Erin. "So you wanted to know about Lawrence Andover?"

"Yes," Erin said. "In fact, we need a favor. We were hoping you could introduce us to him. We think he might know something about the Atkinson sapphire."

"Hmmm," Derrica pondered. "Well, it will have to be during the engagement party. He's taking a long trip to the south of France the next day."

"Do you think you can get us in?" Erin asked eagerly.

"It would be hard to sneak all of you in," Derrica admitted. "Does it have to be everyone?"

The group exchanged confused glances. They hadn't thought about splitting up. Willow took charge.

"Eli needs to go," Willow explained. "He's Lili's brother, and a member of the same secret organization at Atkinson that Lawrence was a part of. If Mr. Andover knows anything about the sapphire, we're hoping he might open up to Eli."

Ryan jumped in. "And Willow and I should be there," he said. Willow looked at him in surprise, and he smiled.

"Are you sure we should all be seen together? Isn't your uncle getting suspicious that you're hanging out with us?" Jasmine asked. "I mean, he seems to have eyes everywhere, you know?"

Ryan shook his head. "I happened to mention that we were doing some field research to get ready for Nationals, to throw him off track, so we can meet with Mr. Andover without drawing attention to ourselves, no problem. Aaron is a master of disguise, so we should bring him along, too, just in case. Also, it's probably a good idea to have a history expert."

Isabel eagerly leaned forward, but Willow insisted on taking Erin. "It should be two Jewels and two Rivals," she explained. "It's only fair."

"So what are the rest of us supposed to do?" Jasmine asked.

"Maybe you can keep researching what the treasure might be," Willow said. "We still have no clue and we don't want to waste time looking for an answer."

Jasmine nodded. It wasn't the most fun assignment, but it was still important.

"Now that that's decided," Derrica said, "I'll have to figure out how to get you in. The Andover mansion is beautiful — and huge. Our families have been friends for years, so I know the layout pretty well. Let me think it over and I'll message Erin and let her know. I've got to run now. I'm late for a fitting at Elan's," she said as she stood up.

Lili's eyes grew wide. "Oh, please post a photo of you wearing Elan's latest creation!"

Derrica laughed. "I will, darling. I'll be in touch. Ta-ta!" She floated out of the café.

Veronica shook her head in disbelief. "She is exactly the same as she is on television. And I thought all reality shows were fake!"

The following Saturday, Eli, Willow, Erin, Ryan, and Aaron met at Ryan's house, which turned out to be within walking distance of the Andover mansion. The mansion, built of red stone, was impressive, and Willow quickly counted over thirty windows in the front of the house. It had a huge front lawn and a circular driveway, complete with a fountain in the middle.

Erin read from her phone. "Derrica said to go to the French doors off the library at four p.m. Then we're supposed to walk around to the back of the house, and the library will be located to our left. Derrica will let us in and bring us to Andover for a meeting."

Guests were already driving up and valets were parking their cars for them. The team decided to walk on the far side of the lawn, which had a row of trees planted next to the driveway, so as not to draw any attention to themselves.

They rounded the house and came to the back, where they saw the gleaming glass French doors, just as Derrica had described. Eli reached his hand to the doorknob and turned it, but the door was locked.

"Did Derrica forget?" Aaron asked, panicked.

If Derrica didn't come through, they would miss their chance to talk to Mr. Andover!

A moment later, the handle of the door turned slowly. Derrica poked her head out. "Just in time!" she said in a loud whisper. "Mr. Andover is in the library."

The group exchanged excited glances. Answers to all their questions about the sapphire could be waiting for them just on the other side of that door!

Chapter Eight

They walked into a large room that still felt cozy despite its size, due to the burgundy carpet on the floor, the dark leather armchairs in front of the fireplace, and the tall mahogany bookcases that stretched from floor to ceiling and filled every inch of wall space. Sitting in one of the chairs was a thin man with a lined face and neatly combed, wavy white hair. He wore a tuxedo and had a plaid blanket on his lap.

"Lawrence, these are the students who wanted to meet you," Derrica said, motioning to them.

"Come in, come in," he said, and it was hard to read his mood. He wasn't smiling, but he didn't sound unfriendly, either. "Hope you don't mind standing. Or the fire, either, for that matter. I know it's late in the spring, but it still feels like winter in my bones."

Derrica stepped back and Willow, Erin, Eli, Ryan, and Aaron awkwardly gathered around Mr. Andover.

"It's nice to meet you, Mr. Andover," Willow said politely. "And thank you for having us."

"It's a good excuse to hide in here for a bit longer," the man replied. "These parties are so terribly boring. A nap is more exciting. But I suppose talking to you will have to do. What is it you all wanted? Derrica didn't say."

"Well, I'm Ryan Atkinson," Ryan began, carefully emphasizing his last name.

Mr. Andover's face brightened. "You're my old friend Charlie's grandson, aren't you? My goodness, I miss that old boy. So do you and your friends go to the school?"

"Yes. And Aaron and Eli do, too," Ryan said, pointing to the other boys.

"And we go to Martha Washington," Erin offered.

"A fine school," Mr. Andover said with a nod. "My, I remember the pranks we used to play on those girls. Had them convinced a ghost was haunting their dining hall! Those were the days."

The old man was smiling now, and he had a distant look in his eyes. Willow and Ryan exchanged glances. He had mentioned "pranks." They were both thinking the same thing. This might be a good time to mention the Memento Mori.

"That's what we came to see you about, sir," Ryan said. "We had some questions about one of the pranks played by the Memento Mori."

"And how do you know about that?" Mr. Andover asked, narrowing his eyes.

Eli stepped forward. "I'm a member, sir," he said. "I saw your name in the roster."

Mr. Andover nodded approvingly. "So, what did you have to do to get in?"

"Well, I had to run Arthur Atkinson's boxer shorts up a flagpole," Eli admitted, blushing a little.

To everyone's surprise, Mr. Andover let out a huge guffaw. He laughed and laughed until Derrica ran up and patted him on the back.

"Lawrence, are you all right?" she asked.

"Better than I have been in years," he replied, wiping away tears. "Oh boy, that's rich. What a classic! I wish I could have seen it. Did you take a picture?"

Eli shook his head. "I was too nervous."

Ryan tapped the screen of his phone and then held it out to Mr. Andover. "It's all over the Internet. See?"

The old man chuckled. "Couldn't have happened to a better person. Ryan, your uncle was always a mean little child. My guess is he's grown up to be a nasty man."

Ryan nodded. "You could say that," he replied, a little sadly.

Mr. Andover took a deep breath. "So. What was your question about the Memento Mori?"

Ryan looked at Eli and gave a small nod. It would be better if Eli asked, since Mr. Andover seemed to like his prank so much.

"Well, it's like this," Eli said, a little nervously. "We need to find the Atkinson sapphire. And we think that maybe the Memento Mori took it as a prank when you were in it."

Mr. Andover eyed Eli for a moment without saying anything. The quiet seemed to drag on for a long time. Finally, he began to speak softly.

"It was so long ago," Mr. Andover said. "But silence is most precious to the Memento Mori. I do not think I could betray that trust, even now."

"I know," Eli said. "But, sir, I read the handbook. Doesn't it also say that the members of the Memento Mori live by a code to do what is right? In this case, telling us about the sapphire is the right thing to do." Eli went on to explain Arthur Atkinson's scheming and how he had tricked a bunch of kids into stealing jewels for him. Mr. Andover's face grew grave as he listened to Eli's account of Arthur's actions. "So, if you tell us what you know about the sapphire, sir, you can help stop him," Eli concluded.

Mr. Andover nodded thoughtfully. "What a bright young man you are. A credit to the Memento Mori, for sure," he said. "Very well. I shall come clean, for the common good."

Eli and the others anxiously waited for him to continue. What did Mr. Andover know?

"Yes, the Memento Mori took the sapphire," he said. "As a prank, just as you have guessed. But the hubbub it caused scared us. There was even talk of bringing in the FBI! So we hid it, and vowed never to speak of it."

The kids all looked at one another, excited. Their guess was right!

"Thank you for telling us," Willow said.

Mr. Andover's voice grew sad. "My Memento Mori brothers are all gone now. I am the last. And the sapphire should be returned to the school, after all. It's only right."

"That's exactly what we plan to do," Ryan said quickly. "The sapphire belongs back at Atkinson."

"Can you tell us where it's hidden?" Willow asked eagerly.

"I wish I could," Mr. Andover said. "But Bobby's the one who hid it. We decided only one of us should know, for safety. And he's pushing up daisies now."

Willow felt like a deflated balloon. They had come so close — only to lose the trail!

"Except . . ." Mr. Andover said slowly. "I remember now. Walter said that Bobby would have to leave some kind of clue, in case anything ever happened to him, so the rest of us could figure it out."

"And do you remember what it was?" Erin asked.

Mr. Andover quickly stood up and surprised them all by moving swiftly along the bookcases.

"It's here somewhere," he said. Then he pulled out an old leather-bound notebook. "Ah, got it!"

"The clue?" Ryan asked.

"It's my journal from 1949," the old man replied. "Hmm . . . let's see. Here it is! 'The first clue is in the painting in the library.'"

"What painting?" Ryan asked.

"And what library?" followed Willow.

"Atkinson Library, I'm sure," Mr. Andover said thoughtfully. "As for the painting, I don't remember. And I didn't write it down, either. Probably why I got all those Cs in school. I was a terrible note taker. I'm sorry."

"Don't be," Erin said quickly. "This is a big help. Now we know where to start looking."

"It's my pleasure," Mr. Andover said, smiling at the young faces assembled before him. "I haven't had this much fun in a long time. If I remember anything else, I'll let Derrica know."

"Thank you so much," Willow said.

"And you tell me if you find the sapphire, will you?" Mr. Andover asked.

"Of course," Ryan promised.

"Wonderful," said Mr. Andover. "And now, before you go, I need you to do one more thing for me."

"What's that?" Eli asked.

Mr. Andover grinned. "Can you show me that picture of the flagpole again?"

Chapter Nine

"So let me get this straight," Jasmine said. "We have to look at all of the paintings in the Atkinson Library for some clue . . . and we don't even know what it is? How many paintings are there?"

After meeting Lawrence Andover, Willow, Erin, and the others met up with the rest of the Jewels and Rivals at Pizza Paradise in Hallytown. They all sat at a large round table, sharing two pizzas and discussing what had happened.

"Dozens," Veronica answered flatly.

"That will take forever!" Isabel wailed.

"Maybe not," Lili said, and everyone looked at her. "I mean, Memento Mori is also a term to describe a style of art. You know, stuff with skulls, mostly. So maybe the clue is in a Memento Mori painting."

"That's genius!" Erin cried.

Aaron looked excited. "I bet I know where the clue is! There's this old painting in the library of a skull on a table next to a vase with a blossoming rose in it."

"It's worth checking out," Willow said.

Ryan nodded. "And at least we know where to start."

Jasmine frowned. "Won't it look suspicious if we march into the library and start examining the painting?"

Ryan grinned. "Not when you can get in anytime you want."

The next morning, Ryan opened the door to the library at Atkinson Preparatory School.

"So you have a key to every building at the school?" Willow asked. She sounded impressed.

"It's one of the perks of being an Atkinson," Ryan said. "You never know when I might need to study on a Sunday morning."

"Or look for a painting without anyone bothering you," Erin piped up.

The library was deserted, which was just perfect. Ryan flipped a switch and the overhead fluorescent lights flickered on.

Erin let out a whistle. "Man, no wonder you guys do so good at quiz bowl. This place is awesome."

The library looked like Lawrence Andover's times ten. In the center of the room was the reading area, filled with gleaming wood desks that featured brass reading lamps at each seat. Thousands of books were shelved on rows of antique wooden shelves, not the industrial metal ones found in the Martha Washington Library.

"It is," Veronica agreed. "And it's so quiet, even on a regular day."

"The painting is over by the Mystery section," Aaron said, sprinting ahead of everyone.

"How fitting," Jasmine said dryly.

Aaron led them to a painting on the wall that was just as he had described. A gray, cracked skull sat on a brown wood table. Next to it, a rose sat in a clear glass vase.

"It's always been one of my favorites," he said, looking up at it with a smile. "It's really cool, right?"

"Cool but creepy," Lili said.

"It is hideous," Isabel said with a derisive sniff. "Can we please stop admiring it and start looking for the clue?"

Ryan reached up and took the painting off the wall.

"Are you sure we can do that?" Jasmine asked.

"Nobody's watching," Ryan pointed out. "Come on, let's get a better look."

He brought the painting to one of the reading tables and turned on the light. After further inspection, Lili noted it was an oil painting. In addition to the skull, tabletop, and vase with the rose, there was a signature on the bottom right.

"It looks like the name Hall," Aaron said. "But I've never come across a painter by that name who's associated with this style."

"Then maybe the name of the painter is the clue," Willow guessed. "Maybe the clue is that the sapphire is in the hall."

"Which hall?" Isabel asked. "There are hundreds of halls here."

"It could be, like, the main hall," Erin suggested.

"Maybe, but where?" Veronica asked.

Aaron picked up the painting. "Let's see what's on the back."

He turned it over to reveal an aged piece of brown paper on the back of the frame.

"Rats," he said with a frown. "I thought there'd be a map or something."

"There *is* something," Lili said, pointing. "Look!"

In the top left corner of the paper was a tiny skull drawn in black ink.

Ryan ran his hand over the symbol. "There's something under there," he said. Then he ran to the librarian's desk and picked up a pair of scissors.

"You can't cut it up!" Jasmine said in horror.

"I'm not hurting the painting, just the paper," Ryan assured her. "Watch."

He carefully sliced open the paper underneath the skull, then reached in and pulled out a small, folded piece of paper.

"Oh my gosh, this is so exciting!" Lili squealed.

Ryan opened it up. "It's a map," he said. "It looks like the grounds of Atkinson."

"It's got to lead to the sapphire," Willow said.

Ryan nodded. "Maybe. There's a line tracing out a route, and it starts here in the library. Let's go."

They left the library and followed Ryan across the grounds to the school's main building. He opened the door and led them past the auditorium, and then made several turns into various hallways. Finally, he stopped in front of a closed door.

"That's funny," he said. "The map says this leads to the basement, but I didn't know there was an entrance to the basement here."

He opened the door to reveal a shallow, empty closet.

"See what I mean?" Ryan asked.

Aaron tapped on the back of the closet, and a hollow sound echoed back at him.

"I bet you there's a staircase behind here," he said. "It doesn't feel like a wall."

"Ooh, it's a secret entrance!" Lili said.

"Well, we can't use scissors to cut our way through," Isabel said.

"We don't have to," Erin argued. She stepped into the closet and felt around the edges of the back wall. She pulled at a corner and a large sheet of plywood came off, revealing a dark staircase beyond.

Everyone stared in amazement. Even Erin looked surprised.

"Wow, I wasn't actually sure that would work."

Willow, Aaron, and Ryan helped Erin move the sheet of wood outside the closet. Isabel nervously peered down into the darkness.

"We should not do this without a flashlight," she said.

"It's cool," Ryan said. "I have a flashlight app on my phone."

Willow grinned at him. "Me, too."

"I'll take the lead, and you can head up the rear," Ryan said, moving toward the opening in the wall.

"I can take the lead," Willow offered.

"You could, but I have the map," Ryan said with a grin, and then he headed down the staircase.

Aaron, Veronica, and Isabel followed Ryan, and then Erin took the lead for the Jewels, followed by Lili, Jasmine, and finally Willow.

Ryan's phone illuminated just a foot or two in front of him, and Willow's light bounced off Lily's shoulders, casting spooky shadows on the dusty brick walls.

"According to the map, we go straight," Ryan called back to the others. "Just keep moving and you'll be fine."

"This is ridiculous," said Isabel as she stepped off the last stair. "I am getting dust all over my . . . *Eeeeeekkkkkkkkk!*"

Isabel's ear-splitting shriek echoed through the basement. She rushed forward, nearly knocking over Veronica.

"Something touched my leg!" she cried. "It is probably a hairy tarantula! Or a rat!"

Lili, Erin, and Willow quickly backed up on the stairs. Aaron and Veronica stepped away from Isabel. Ryan flashed his light around Isabel's feet.

"I don't see anything," he reported.

Erin spoke up. "Oh gosh, look at that. I must have accidentally dropped my fuzzy pen. Sorry, Isabel."

She held up a novelty pen with googly eyes and furry orange hair. Isabel looked furious.

"I do not understand why we have to work with these immature girls," she said resentfully.

"Excuse me, but if it weren't for us, you wouldn't have seen the

Memento Mori list or gotten to meet Lawrence Andover, either, for that matter," Erin shot back.

"Can you two please quit it?" Willow called out. "We're, like, just a few feet away from maybe finding the sapphire. We need to focus."

"Oh, I'm focused," Erin said, glaring at Isabel.

Isabel turned her back to Erin. "I am more focused than you."

"Great," Ryan said. He took a few steps forward. "So the map ends at this brick wall."

"And then what?" Aaron asked.

"There are some numbers," Ryan replied. "27X, 15Y."

Willow quickly moved forward. "Those are coordinates, like on a graph or a grid," the Jewels' math expert said excitedly, shining her light on the wall. "See the bricks? What if each one is a point on the coordinates?"

Ryan started to nod excitedly. "So that would be fifteen bricks from the floor, and then twenty-seven bricks in from the left," he said, counting as he talked. "Twenty-five . . . twenty-six . . . twenty-seven!"

Ryan touched the brick. "It's loose!"

"Hold up!" Erin warned. "This is the part where you grab the sapphire, then say, 'So long, suckers!' and escape through some secret passage, right?"

Ryan sighed. "Wrong. I already told you guys that you can trust us."

"That's not good enough," Erin said. "Let Willow move the brick with you."

"Fine," Ryan said impatiently. "Let's just do this."

Willow and Ryan each touched the brick and began to pry it loose. It easily came off in their hands.

"There's something in there!" Willow cried.

Ryan pulled out a black pouch, opened it, and slid the contents into Willow's open palm. His light illuminated a gleaming blue jewel.

"It's the sapphire," he said breathlessly, and the other kids let out a spontaneous cheer.

"We did it!" Erin cried.

"Let's get it back to the library so we can get a closer look," Willow suggested.

"Good idea," said Isabel. "I will be happy to get out of this *base cement*, or whatever you call it."

Ryan gave Willow the pouch. "You should carry it," he said, and Willow smiled.

They went back up the stairs, replaced the fake wall, and made sure to close the closet behind them. Then they hurried back through the deserted halls, across the campus, and returned to the library. Willow took a seat at a table while the others gathered around her. She turned on a reading light and slipped the sapphire out of its pouch.

About an inch in diameter, the round stone had beautiful facets cut into its surface. It was set in what looked like a gold circle with a ring of tiny, creamy white jewels all around it.

"It's a brooch," Jasmine said. "And those are pearls."

She gently picked it up and turned it over. The back of the jewel was open, with the bar of the brooch pin going across.

"Do you see a symbol?" Ryan asked.

"I think so," Jasmine said, pointing. "Look."

"We should take a picture of it," Ryan said, holding up his phone.

"I wouldn't do that if I were you."

The sound of a familiar voice caused them all to freeze. Arthur Atkinson was standing in the library doorway, an evil grin on his face.

"Please be so kind as to step away from my sapphire," he said.

Chapter Ten

"I knew this was a setup!" Erin yelled.

Arthur Atkinson laughed. "It was, but not the kind you think," he said with a grin, his tall frame looming over them. "When my nephew here announced that he and his friends were no longer going to play my little game, I suspected he would go behind my back and try to find the sapphire. Getting you to help him was his own idea. Smart. But unfortunately, Ryan, you weren't smart enough to make sure I wasn't following you."

Ryan's cheeks flushed red and he looked down at the table. Erin realized how difficult his relationship with his uncle must be, and that made her sympathize with Ryan. But she was angrier than ever. She quickly grabbed the sapphire.

"If you think we're handing this over, you're crazy," Erin said.

"On the contrary, I am thinking quite clearly," Atkinson replied, his voice as smooth as oil. "The sapphire belongs to Atkinson Preparatory

School. I am the director of the school. If you don't turn it over to me, I will simply call the police."

"You'd better give it to him, Erin," Jasmine whispered. At one time, the police suspected that Jasmine might have stolen the Martha Washington diamond. She didn't want to go through that terrible experience again.

"Call them," Erin said, keeping her eyes locked with Arthur Atkinson's. "We'll tell them the whole story."

"You could," Arthur Atkinson said. "But then they'd have to believe you. They didn't believe you when you said the Rivals had stolen the diamond."

"Listen to him," Ryan said. "It's not worth it."

Willow turned to Erin, and her face was serious. "I hate to say it, but Ryan's right."

Erin's grip on the sapphire was so tight that her knuckles were white. She hated to give it up, but she knew she had to. Reluctantly, she loosened her grip and handed it to Aaron.

"You do it," she said. "I don't want to go near that creep."

Aaron walked over to his principal and gave him the sapphire.

"Thank you," Arthur Atkinson said with a slick grin.

"You should," Erin said. "You couldn't have done it without us."

Atkinson slipped the sapphire into his jacket pocket and left the library without another word.

"Well, that's it," Jasmine said glumly, sinking into a chair. "Game over."

"Maybe not," Lili said, and everyone turned to look at her. She put a finger to her lips and slowly held up her right hand.

"No way!" Erin whispered.

Lili had drawn the symbol from the back of the sapphire on her palm!

Chapter Eleven

"Lili, close your hand!" Willow hissed. "We don't know if Atkinson is watching us somehow even now."

"Let's get out of here, fast," Ryan agreed.

When they got outside, they looked around to make sure Arthur Atkinson was nowhere around.

"Let's go to the Hallytown Community Center," she suggested, and then explained to the Rivals, "My mom works there."

"That should be safe," Ryan said.

"The bus to Hallytown is just a few blocks away," Willow pointed out. "We can text our parents and tell them we're studying there."

Twenty minutes later, they stepped off the local bus in front of the community center. Cheerful yellow daffodils covered the front lawn. Inside, they stopped by the main office, where Willow's mom was seated behind a desk covered with photos of Willow and her brothers.

"Willow!" Mrs. Albern looked surprised to see her daughter. "But I thought you all were studying at Atkinson."

"Well . . . Ryan forgot his key," Willow said, thinking quickly. "I was wondering if we could use the meeting room, if it's open."

"Of course!" Willow's mom replied with a smile. "It's nice to see you two teams working together. That's true sportsmanship."

"Yeah, we're practically all best friends now," Erin piped up, casting a wicked glance at Isabel, who frowned.

"Well, enjoy your studying," Mrs. Albern said. "We close in a couple of hours."

Willow led them to the meeting room, and they all took seats at the round table.

"We should check for bugs before we do anything," Jasmine said.

Erin glared at the Rivals. "Oh yeah, that's right. You guys bugged us once before."

"That was my uncle's idea," Ryan said defensively.

"All the more reason to check now," Willow said, and they all looked through their bags and clothes for anything suspicious — but found nothing.

"Okay, Lili," Erin said. "Let's see that hand."

Lili opened her palm and placed it on the table where everyone could see. The symbol she had drawn was three squares of different sizes. Their corners were touching so that the three linked sides of the squares formed a triangle.

"It's the Pythagorean theorem!" Willow and Ryan burst out at the same time.

"Let me guess," Erin said. "That's a math thing, right?"

Willow nodded. "Geometry. It's, like, a diagram that explains this theory. You see these two squares here? If you add up the areas of these two, they'll equal the area of the big square."

"Wow. My brain hurts just thinking about it," Aaron quipped. "So what does that have to do with the other clues?"

"Wait a second, that's right!" Jasmine said. "We've only seen the clue on the back of the diamond. But you guys know the clues on the back of the emerald and the ruby, right?"

"We do," Veronica replied. "But they don't make any sense. We were hoping the clue on the sapphire would shed some light on the first three."

Jasmine took out the sketchbook she always carried with her and opened it up. "Whenever we found something written about the jewels, they're in the same order: ruby, diamond, emerald, sapphire. So we should lay the clues out the same way."

"Good idea," Veronica said. "The first one should be the number one-ten followed by a little circle. That was on the ruby."

"And E-fifty was on the diamond," Willow added.

"The third clue contains a letter and a number, too," Ryan added. "It's N–two hundred."

"And then we have the symbol," Jasmine said, copying it into the book. It felt strange and exciting to see all the clues together after searching for them for so long.

Willow frowned at the clues. "That doesn't seem to clear things up at all."

"So wait a second," Erin said. "You mean you guys have had the first three clues for weeks and haven't figured out anything about them yet?"

"It is not that easy," Isabel said defensively.

"But, guys, that's a good thing," Jasmine pointed out. "That means that Arthur Atkinson is as clueless as we are. And if he needed us to find the sapphire for him, then he can't be that bright. No offense, Ryan."

"It's cool," Ryan said. "Uncle Arthur is not famous for his brains in my family. Dad says they let him be the director of the school just so he doesn't mess up the family's big companies."

Erin rolled her eyes. "Nice. Stick him in charge of a bunch of kids."

"He might not be smart, but he can hire people who are," Ryan reminded them all. "So we'd better try to figure the clues out first."

"Maybe it's a mathematical formula," Willow suggested. She opened up the calculator on her phone and began typing in numbers.

"The N and E could stand for directions — north and east," Erin pointed out.

"We thought of that already," Isabel said with a sniff. "But it is no good without knowing more about the location."

"Maybe they're addresses," Lili suggested. "Have you checked addresses in the DC area that match? You know, like one hundred North Street or something like that?"

Ryan nodded. "There are lots of streets like that. It's hard to narrow it down."

"And that still doesn't explain the Pythagorean symbol at the end," Willow added.

They all sighed at once, followed by an uncomfortable silence. Then Veronica's wristwatch began to beep.

"Oh no! We've got quiz bowl practice!" she cried.

"You guys practice on a Sunday?" Erin asked.

"We practice all the time," Isabel said. "Which is why we always beat you."

"Not always," Erin shot back. The Jewels had beaten the Rivals the last time they'd gone head-to-head.

"We'll have to finish this argument some other time," Ryan said, standing up. "In the meantime, let's keep working on the clues. We can text each other if we figure out anything."

"And how do we keep your uncle from spying on us in the meantime?" Erin asked.

Ryan frowned. "I don't know. Let me check my room at home. Maybe he bugged me there. But our texts should be safe."

"My mom's going to be outside in five minutes to get us," Veronica said, looking up from her cell phone. "We'd better go."

The Rivals left, leaving the Jewels alone in the meeting room.

"You know what I'm thinking?" Willow asked.

"That we need to figure out the clues before Arthur Atkinson does?" Jasmine asked.

Willow shook her head. "No, that we need to study, too. I don't want to fall behind in quiz bowl just because we're solving the jewel-thieving mystery of the century!"

Chapter Twelve

"Achoo!" Erin's loud sneeze ricocheted through Hallytown High School's auditorium, causing several people, including Willow and Jasmine, to jump.

"Hold still!" Lili scolded behind the curtain as she once again patted Erin's face with a large cosmetics puff. Drifts of powder settled in Erin's reddish-blond hair, and she shook her head to get it off. Lili sighed. "Honestly, Erin, don't you want to be camera ready?"

After two days of marathon study sessions, the Jewels were ready to compete in a quiz bowl tournament that would be broadcast on a local cable channel. They were competing in the local high school's auditorium because of its A/V capabilities.

Erin folded her arms in front of her and stuck her tongue out at Lili. "The camera will just have to deal with my face as it is," she said.

Lili shot an exasperated look at Erin before hopefully offering up her makeup bag to Willow and Jasmine.

"No way!" Jasmine said, while Willow fiercely shook her head.

"At least we're all wearing my new and improved T-shirts!" Lili said, pointing to her top. It was the same red shirt with the words "Jewels Rule" stenciled on the front that the girls had worn the last time they had beaten the Rivals, but Lili had added brightly colored fake gems to the shirts.

"They were missing something." Lili beamed. "Now they're perfect!"

"They brought us luck last time we faced the Rivals," Jasmine added. "It will be weird competing against them today. After getting to know them and all."

Willow nodded. "I'm really surprised the Rivals even agreed to do it. It's only for fun. A win won't count toward our stats, and the Rivals only play to better their national standing."

"It's the new and improved Rivals," Erin joked in a fake commercial announcer's voice. "Now twenty-five percent softer and more likable."

The girls erupted into laughter as Ms. Keatley hurried over.

"Girls," she said in a loud whisper. "They're getting ready to start. We have to be quiet. In fact, there's a classroom we can wait in until it's our turn."

The girls followed Ms. Keatley out of the auditorium.

"The high school teams will go first," she explained once they entered the hall and walked toward a classroom door. "Then it will be you versus the Rivals, the top two middle school teams from the entire county." Ms. Keatley beamed with pride as she said this. "They are going to film all the matches today, but each one will air as its own episode."

Standing in front of the door was Mr. Haverford, the Rivals' advisor. His eyes lit up when he saw Ms. Keatley.

"Just the person I was looking for!" he said. "Do you have a second to talk about Nationals?"

"Sure." Ms. Keatley smiled at him. "Girls, go inside, find a seat, and relax."

They walked into the classroom to find Ryan, Veronica, Isabel, and Aaron, wearing their blue Atkinson uniforms. Willow hurried over to Ryan. "Did you find any bugs in your room?"

Ryan shook his head. "No. But I'm going to keep looking. My uncle has access to some pretty high-tech gear."

Aaron walked up to talk with Ryan and Willow, and the other Jewels took a seat. Erin gave a smile and wave to Veronica, who had her earbuds in. She smiled back, but it was clear that her pre–quiz bowl routine included psyching up with music, not chitchatting.

Lili held up her makeup bag again and looked at Jasmine with her big brown eyes.

"Uh-oh! She's doing puppy dog eyes," Erin warned Jasmine. "Look away! Look away!"

"How about just a smidge of lip gloss?" Lili pleaded.

Jasmine sighed as she gave in. "Fine."

"There is no resisting Lili when she does that," Erin said as Lili eagerly dug through her bag.

Erin riffled through her own backpack and pulled out some Martha Washington books that she had checked out from the school library weeks ago. She flipped through them one more time, hoping to find something — anything — that might shed light on the clues that were etched into the gems. As she began to read, she felt someone sit down in the seat next to her. She looked up from her book — it was Isabel!

"I've been meaning to get this one," Isabel said, her green eyes devouring the cover eagerly. "May I see it?"

"Sure," Erin said in surprise. She still felt on guard when it came to Isabel, but she handed the book over.

Isabel studied it carefully. "I love how Martha is portrayed as young and beautiful here. So many people know her only as a frumpy old lady."

"If you like this book, you should see the others I have." Erin couldn't help sharing. She loved history and loved to talk to other history enthusiasts, although she never in a million years thought she'd be talking with Isabel like this. She reached into her backpack and pulled out some of the older and rarer books about Martha. "Our library has an amazing collection of books about her."

Isabel pulled a folder from her own backpack and took from it a photocopy of an old letter. "This is a letter written from George Washington to Martha. It's one of only five letters between them that survived. Martha burned all of their correspondence after George's death."

Erin nodded. "She wanted to keep things private. Who could blame her? They were the equivalent of movie stars back then. Everyone wanted to know all their personal business. When I found an original letter she wrote, I was so totally excited!"

Isabel's eyes grew wide. "An original letter?"

Erin found herself telling Isabel the story of how the Jewels discovered a letter from Martha to a person they thought might be Abigail Adams — and how Martha described the four jewels.

"That's what first made us realize the ruby was part of something bigger," Erin explained, despite it feeling really weird to talk to Isabel like this. "Then we found Martha's diary, and that's what led us to the Townsend desk at the Met and the diamond."

Isabel clasped her hands and stared into space, looking thoughtful. "You know, we have a letter, too. But it's not from Martha Washington. It's *to* her."

"Do you have it with you?" Erin asked excitedly.

Isabel reached into her bag again. "Yes, I have a copy on my tablet." But before she could pull it out, Ms. Keatley stuck her head in the room. "It's showtime, girls! Are you ready?"

The Jewels and the Rivals stood up at the same time. Ryan looked at Willow and gave her an awkward grin, not his usual smug smile. Willow felt a momentary feeling of surprise, but she understood how he was feeling. This would be the first time they'd be competing as friends and not enemies — but only one team could win.

Chapter Thirteen

"This match goes to the Atkinson Prep Rivals!" announced the quiz bowl moderator.

The audience applauded. The Rivals high-fived, while the Jewels huddled together on the side of the stage. It was hard not to be disappointed. Nationals was only weeks away, and losing to the Rivals now seemed like a bad omen — and a step backward.

"We may have lost, but we played great," Willow consoled them. Normally she hated losing, but it had been a close contest, and they had performed well. "The match had to go into a tiebreaker and everything. We lost by only one question."

They shook hands with the Rivals and rushed off the stage. For the first time ever, the Rivals didn't smirk or tease them. In fact, they only had one thing on their minds.

"We need to get together and figure out our next move," Aaron whispered to Jasmine as they left the stage.

"Agreed," Jasmine said. Erin overheard them and jumped in. "Isabel needs to show me something. It could be important."

When they got offstage, they found Principal Frederickson waiting to be the first to greet them. As usual, she was dressed smartly: this time in a navy-blue suit jacket and matching skirt with a crisp white blouse.

"You performed magnificently," she said. "Such a credit to our school."

Willow beamed with pride. "Thanks," she said.

"I can tell that you've been concentrating on your studies . . . and not on other things," the principal said, giving them a stern look.

Jasmine cast a nervous glance at Willow. Did Principal Frederickson know that they were still searching for the treasure?

Luckily, Ms. Keatley walked up, and Principal Frederickson politely stepped aside. "Great job, girls," she said as she hugged them. "You have a shot at the Nationals, that's for sure!"

Erin agreed, "You're right, Ms. Keatley, but I'm still bummed. Why don't we invite the Rivals out for pizza to cheer us up?"

Ms. Keatley raised her eyebrows. "Really?" she asked as she looked at each girl. They all smiled and nodded.

"I already made arrangements with your parents to take you out for pizza after the match. I'm just surprised you want the Rivals to come along with us, but if that's what you want," she said, "then I'll ask Josh — I mean, Mr. Haverford."

They crowded into Ms. Keatley's VW Bug and followed Mr. Haverford, who drove the Rivals to Pizza Paradise. It was only a few minutes away from the high school, and soon they were all inside, breathing in the aroma of freshly baked pizza.

"Yum!" Lili said as she sniffed the air.

"Double yum!" Erin cried. "Competing at quiz bowl always makes me hungry."

After ordering, they began to look for somewhere to sit. There was a table for eight in the back of the room.

"Ms. Keatley, may we sit here?" Willow asked. "This is the biggest table."

Ms. Keatley nodded. "Sure, Mr. Haverford and I will sit at this table next to you." She pointed to a two-person booth. Mr. Haverford smiled at Ms. Keatley, and Ms. Keatley blushed.

Jasmine exchanged amused glances with Aaron. Both the Rivals and the Jewels had noticed Mr. Haverford had a huge crush on Ms. Keatley for a while now. She had been completely oblivious, but it looked like she finally might be figuring it out. Ryan laughed as he sat down.

"If they get married and have a family, they can start their own toddler quiz bowl team," Erin joked. "They'll be hard to beat!"

"Maybe for you," Isabel sniffed. Erin felt her cheeks flush, but Isabel quickly apologized. "I'm sorry," she gave a genuine smile. "It's just a bad reflex. You guys almost beat us, I'll admit it."

Veronica, happy over her team's win, wasn't about to count out the Jewels, either. "It was a close match. We're going to have to study extra hard for Nationals if we want to beat you!"

They dug into slices of hot, cheesy pizza, munching away as they talked. Ms. Keatley and Mr. Haverford were deep in conversation at the next table, so the two teams could speak freely.

Isabel began to fill them in on the letter as she got her tablet out. "It's from a Samuel Lindley to Martha Washington. He was a silversmith and he definitely helped her with something. But we haven't been able to get anything useful out of it."

The Jewels exchanged excited glances before Erin spoke up. "Martha mentioned a 'trustworthy jeweler' in her letter to Abigail. Silversmiths and jewelers were the same thing back then, right? Maybe it's the same jeweler?"

Isabel shrugged. "I'll read it to you. Maybe you can find something in it that we missed." She tapped the screen on her tablet and began to read aloud:

" 'To Mrs. Martha Washington

Dear Madam:

It gives me particular pleasure to hear that both you and General Washington are in good health. I am exceedingly obliged to you for your trust in me and promise the items have been set and are well dispersed.

Moreover, I want to assure you of my dedication to the peace and liberty for which we have so long contended. Over time our cause will be victorious. Understandably the strain of war leaves much sorrow. Now is the time to remain ever hopeful. The tumultuous days ahead cannot be avoided, but know I have done everything possible to aid you. Virginia has no British troops upon its soil at this time. Everything points to triumph. Report back when you are able, as I am most eager to hear any news. Night is falling and I bid you good evening. Our only course is to bear our burdens patiently. Never forget that I am your dutiful servant, always.

With great esteem,
Samuel Lindley
Silversmith' "

Jasmine gasped. "It must be the same jeweler from Martha's letter! Remember, she asked the jeweler to set the ruby, diamond, emerald, and sapphire for her. I think Lindley not only set them, but made sure they were separated. Maybe that's what he meant by 'well dispersed.' Martha didn't want all the jewels found together, remember?"

Aaron slumped in his chair. "But there's no hint about where the treasure is hidden," he groaned. "We're no better off than we were before."

"If the treasure was hidden, why didn't he or somebody else get it after the war?" Willow asked. "Or maybe someone did and all this is for nothing."

Isabel shook her head, her short blond hair swinging around her face. "I have done some research on Samuel Lindley. He died in 1780, three years before the war ended."

Veronica leaned forward on the table, her eyes gleaming. "Maybe he took the secret of where the treasure was hidden to the grave with him. It could still be hidden away after all these years."

Ryan nodded. "It's a possibility. But where is it hidden?"

Lili snapped her fingers. "What if there is a code in the note, kind of like a hidden message or something? Like the Memento Mori sent to Eli. Lindley would have wanted Martha to know where the treasure was, right?"

Isabel and Erin both spoke at the same time: "I love codes!" They looked at each other in surprise and everyone burst out laughing.

"Maybe they are long-lost sisters," Aaron joked.

Isabel handed over her tablet to Erin, who grabbed a notebook out of her backpack. "It helps if I write it out line by line. Makes you pay attention to each and every letter."

She began to write as Isabel leaned over her shoulder, watching every letter carefully. "It could be an acrostic puzzle," Isabel suggested eagerly.

Erin continued to write, her lips pursed in concentration. "Maybe, but if so, it's not hidden in the first paragraph."

"What's an acrostic puzzle?" Veronica wondered as the girls worked.

"It's when a recurring feature in the written words spells out a word or message," Aaron, the Rivals' arts and literature expert, explained. "Like the first word of every sentence or paragraph."

Lili nodded in agreement. "It's a form of poetry, too."

Erin dropped her pen and looked at Isabel, who was grinning from ear to ear. "We did it! We did it!" Erin shouted.

Ms. Keatley and Mr. Haverford looked over at them, startled. "What did you do, Erin?" Mr. Haverford asked.

"Um, we ate all the pizza," Erin said quickly. "I'm a lifetime member of the clean plate club so that makes me happy."

The teachers laughed and returned to their conversation.

"What did you find?" Willow asked impatiently.

"The first letter of every sentence in the second paragraph spells out the name of a place," Isabel shared, as Erin held up her notebook.

Moreover, I want to assure you of my dedication to the peace and liberty we have so long contended. Over time our cause will be victorious. Understandably the strain of war leaves much sorrow. Now is the time to remain ever hopeful. The tumultuous days ahead cannot be avoided, but know I have done everything possible to aid you. Virginia has no British troops upon its soil at this time. Everything points to triumph. Report back when you are able, as I am most eager to hear any news. Night is falling and I bid you good evening. Our only course is to bear our burdens patiently. Never forget that I am your dutiful servant, always.

They all leaned over to read it. Jasmine gasped with excitement.

"The treasure is hidden at Mount Vernon!" she cried.

Chapter Fourteen

"Shhh," Willow warned. "What if Arthur Atkinson is listening?"

"I don't blame her. This is amazing," Aaron said. "I mean, it's right there in the letter. Mount Vernon, the famous home of George and Martha Washington."

Excited, Erin bolted out of her chair, knocking it over. "Let's go!" she cried.

Ms. Keatley looked up and frowned. "We're not done eating yet, Erin."

"Oh yeah, right. Sorry!" Erin tried to keep her legs from running out the door. "I'll just sit and wait." She righted her chair and sat back down in it, tapping her feet impatiently.

"Smooth move," Ryan leaned over and whispered.

Lili stuck up for her friend. "But this is big news!"

Erin's feet ricocheted along the floor. "Mount Vernon is not too far from here. We could be there in under an hour!"

"It's nighttime, Erin. Mount Vernon is closed to visitors now," Willow reminded her. "But you're right. We should go and investigate ASAP."

Erin let out a big exhalation of air. Her feet stopped tapping. "Okay. But how do we get there?"

Ryan and Willow exchanged grins, both thinking the same thing. "No problem!" Ryan said. He walked over to the booth Ms. Keatley and Mr. Haverford were sitting in, Willow right behind him.

"We had an idea," Ryan said, smiling. "We were all just talking about how field trips are a great way to study."

"Immersion learning!" Willow chimed in. "It's been working really well for us."

"Learning from experience is highly effective," Ms. Keatley said while Mr. Haverford nodded in agreement.

"To prepare for Nationals, we'd all like to visit Mount Vernon together," Ryan said. "Could we take a field trip?"

"That's a wonderful idea." Mr. Haverford beamed. He looked hopefully at Ms. Keatley. "What do you think? We could take the Atkinson Prep van and all ride down together."

"How about this weekend?" Ms. Keatley replied.

Mr. Haverford opened the calendar on his smartphone. "Does Saturday work for you?"

Ms. Keatley nodded. "It's a date!" she said. As soon as she realized what she had said, her cheeks began to turn red. "I mean, it's a date for us to take our students there, of course."

Mr. Haverford smiled at her. "Of course," he said.

"Yuck!" Ryan whispered in Willow's ear and she giggled.

"I'll be in touch with your parents to get permission slips signed," Ms. Keatley said.

Willow and Ryan returned to their chairs and waited until Ms. Keatley and Mr. Haverford were deep in conversation again before speaking.

"Today is Wednesday," Willow said. "That gives us a couple of days to try to work out the clues from the ruby, diamond, emerald, and sapphire. If we can figure that out, we'll know what to look for when we get to Mount Vernon."

Ryan frowned. "I just thought of something. My uncle's computer calendar gets automatically updated with all field trips. If he sees we're all going to Mount Vernon together, he'll be suspicious. What should we do?"

"Maybe Eli could use his computer wizardry and wipe it off the calendar?" Lili suggested.

"Does he know how to do something like that?" Ryan asked.

"Eli can do anything," Lili said confidently.

"Okay, talk to Eli and let us know what he says," Willow told Lili. "Everyone else, keep researching. If you find anything out, text us."

The next afternoon, Willow sat at her desk in her bedroom, her door shut to keep out her three little brothers. She was trying to study for the quiz bowl Nationals, but her mind kept wandering back to Mount Vernon and the clues etched on the gems. What could they mean?

She let out a big sigh before turning the volume up on the online radio station she was streaming. A little background music always helped her to concentrate. She hummed along as she read the sample math questions Ms. Keatley had given her. Willow was surprised at how much she was beginning to like the Rivals, especially Ryan. But no matter how good friends they might become, she still wanted to beat them at Nationals, and the competition was only a few weeks away. She had to focus!

She managed to work her way through a couple of sample questions before her eyes fell on the map of Mount Vernon Estate she had spread out earlier on her desk. *Hmmm*, she thought, *the main part of the estate is sort of a circle shape*. Her eyes went back to her paper and the next sample question, this one about geometry. She stared at the circle on the page. Circles. It made her think of the first clue etched on the ruby: 110°. If the little circle was a degree mark, it could refer to a point on a circle, like one hundred and ten degrees.

She sat up straight and shut the radio off. *I think I'm on to something*, she thought. She pushed the study papers aside and pulled the map directly in front of her. *If you assume that zero degrees is at the very top center of the map, then one hundred and ten degrees would be* — she ran her finger down the map — *right here!* Her finger had stopped at a point in Mount Vernon Estate right by the path leading to the fruit garden.

She tapped the map excitedly. If they started at this spot, the other clues might lead to the exact location of the treasure. Maybe, just *maybe*, she could be right! Willow grabbed her phone.

I think I've got it, she texted to all of her friends — even the Rivals. *I know where we should look when we get 2 MV!*

Chapter Fifteen

The next day after school Willow met with Ryan at Café X to talk about her discovery. She spread the map of Mount Vernon out on the table and showed Ryan how she came to her conclusion.

"So if the small circle after one hundred and ten is a degree mark, it would put us right here." She pointed to the path leading to the fruit garden.

Ryan let out a low whistle and sat back in his chair. "Wow. I never would have thought of that. I'm impressed, Willow."

Willow smiled proudly. "It's not for sure. We'll have to figure out what the E-fifty and N–two hundred mean. And then there's that Pythagorean symbol on the sapphire."

"The E and N could stand for east and north," Ryan suggested. "So maybe you need to walk that number of feet or paces in either direction."

Willow smacked a palm to her forehead. "Duh! Why didn't I think of that?"

"If you hadn't thought of the degrees, I never would have gotten that idea," Ryan said. "We're a good team. That's why I wanted your help."

They both grinned at each other for a moment before Willow said, "I talked to Lili. Eli said he couldn't delete the field trip from Atkinson's calendar, but he could move it to a different date. He's going to put it to next Saturday, not this one."

Ryan frowned. "I hope that throws him off the trail, at least for a little while. Even so, we'll have to be careful and keep an eye out for him."

Willow took out her phone and started texting. "I'm going to send a group message out to everyone to let them know what we've figured out so far. Too bad no one else could make it. Jasmine has a dance class, Lili is at an art club meeting, and Erin was forced into going to her sister Mary Ellen's ice-skating competition."

"It's hard to remember sometimes, but we do have actual lives outside all of this jewels drama." Ryan sighed. "I guess life will get back to normal once we find the treasure."

But he didn't look happy about it, and neither did Willow. They both laughed out loud after noticing each other's sad faces.

"It has been fun," Willow admitted.

"And exciting!" Ryan added.

Willow's phone beeped when she received a text message. "It's from Erin," she explained to Ryan. "She said she has a lead on the clue on the sapphire. She'll tell us on the trip to Mount Vernon. "

"Every last bit of information helps," Ryan said solemnly. "We have to do anything we can to find the treasure before my uncle does!"

Saturday morning dawned sunny and bright, with only a few fluffy white clouds dotting the sky. The Jewels and Ms. Keatley stood in front of Martha Washington School, waiting for the Rivals to pick them up.

"Today's the big day," Lili whispered to the others so Ms. Keatley wouldn't overhear her. "I wonder what we'll find!"

Jasmine bit her lip. "I don't want to get my hopes up, but I have such a good feeling. It's like I can just tell something is out there, waiting for us to find it."

"No matter what, we'll know we tried our best," Willow whispered back to her friends.

Erin nodded. "If the Jewels can't do it, no one can!"

A shiny white van with blue lettering that read "Atkinson Preparatory School" pulled into the driveway. Mr. Haverford parked the car and hopped out, walking toward Ms. Keatley with a big smile on his face.

"Your chariot awaits," he said with a bow. The girls stifled giggles as Ms. Keatley got into the front passenger seat. Mr. Haverford slid the large van doors open for them and the girls climbed inside. Isabel, Veronica, and Aaron sat in the rear row. Ryan sat in the middle and scooted over to make room for Willow and Jasmine, while Erin and Lili took the front row.

After buckling up, Erin leaned over her seat and spoke in a low voice to the others.

"I can't believe it took me this long to figure it out," Erin said. "The symbol on the sapphire — the Pythagorean theorem — it's a symbol the Masons use!"

"Of course!" Isabel added. "And George Washington was a Mason."

"What's a Mason?" Veronica wondered.

"It's the name for someone who is a member of the Freemasons, a fraternal organization for men, first formed in the sixteenth century. It still exists today," Isabel explained. "There's lots of mystery surrounding the early Masons, including hidden symbols on everything from the dollar bill to the Capitol building."

Aaron frowned. "That's interesting and all, but how does it help us understand the clues?"

Ryan shook his head. "It doesn't, but maybe it will mean something when we get to Mount Vernon."

Jasmine rubbed the side of her nose nervously, while Veronica twisted anxiously in her seat. After what seemed like forever, the van pulled into a parking lot at Mount Vernon. The Rivals and the Jewels exchanged excited glances. It was time to find out if they had guessed right.

Ms. Keatley's eyes gleamed as they walked to the main entrance. "We're in for a treat!" she said. "Dozens of the original buildings used in the Washingtons' time still stand today. It's truly like stepping back in history!"

Their first stop was the orientation center, where they watched an exciting movie about George Washington. It was hard to concentrate, though, knowing what lay ahead. Erin drummed her fingers impatiently on the arm of her chair. "Did you and Isabel figure out how to distract them?" Willow leaned over and whispered to her, nodding at Ms. Keatley and Mr. Haverford.

Erin gave a huge grin before answering. "No problemo. We got a great idea on how to do it from the Martha Washington book we were looking at the other day."

They left the visitor's center and joined the crowds of tourists walking down the pathway, admiring the green lawns and early spring flowers. Willow sprang into action.

"Since the weather is so warm today, can we start in the fruit gardens and work our way back?" Willow asked Ms. Keatley.

Their advisor shrugged her shoulders and looked at Mr. Haverford. "That's fine with me. In fact, it's a good plan. We'll beat the crowds that way, because it looks like most everyone else is heading toward the upper gardens first. Is that okay with you?" she asked Mr. Haverford.

He grinned at Willow. "Excellent suggestion."

They started out on the path that looped around the estate, heading toward the fruit gardens. When they reached the middle of the path, they had a perfect view of the Mount Vernon mansion across the large lawn. It was an impressive white brick house with a red roof and majestic columns.

"Beautiful," Lili said, her eyes wide as she took in the structure. She felt like sitting on the grass and sketching the mansion, but knew they were there on a mission. She sighed. Maybe another time.

Ms. Keatley and Mr. Haverford walked slowly behind the kids. They were deep in conversation and Ryan gave Willow a wink. This would make putting their plan into action a lot easier!

They passed the paddock that housed sheep, horses, and — a little farther up — pigs. Lili sniffed the air. "It smells like Eli's gym socks." She pinched her nose.

Willow had the map open in her hands when she stopped suddenly. "We're close," she whispered. Ryan nodded at Erin and Isabel. It was time for them to distract Ms. Keatley and Mr. Haverford while the others went in search of the treasure.

"Marie Antoinette was way more beautiful than Martha Washington!" Isabel whirled toward Erin, shouting. "Martha was an old frump!"

Erin snorted. "And you call yourself a history expert? Everyone knows now that Martha was not only a shrewd estate manager, but really pretty. Marie Antoinette may have been cute, but she wasn't that bright."

"Ha!" Isabel yelled. "Of course you're going to side with the American. What you know about French history I can fit in my little finger." She jabbed her pinky menacingly into Erin's face.

The two carried on as Mr. Haverford and Ms. Keatley rushed over. He looked at Ms. Keatley and shook his head. "Arguments over history? I didn't know that refereeing them was part of our job description."

It was the perfect distraction. While the two advisors tried to calm Erin and Isabel's fake feud, Willow ran toward the edge of the fruit garden that matched the hundred and ten degree point on the map. Jasmine, Lili, and the rest of the Rivals quickly followed behind her.

If they were right, the treasure was only two hundred fifty paces away!

Chapter Sixteen

Erin and Isabel could still be heard shouting in the distance when Willow skidded to a halt. "This is the spot that's equal to one hundred ten degrees on the estate map," she said, panting slightly.

"Two hundred paces north!" Ryan said at the exact moment Jasmine said "Fifty paces east!" They exchanged confused glances.

"We've got to go east first, then north," Jasmine quickly explained. "In all the references to the jewels we've ever found in letters or diaries they are listed in the same order: ruby, diamond, emerald, and sapphire. So if one hundred ten degrees from the ruby is the first clue, then the E-fifty from the diamond has to be the second," she insisted.

"Smart thinking," Ryan agreed.

Veronica nodded. "We can always come back and try it the other way if it's a dead end."

Willow took the lead and began to measure steady, even paces with her feet, which took them on the path that led into the fruit garden.

"Is this where George Washington chopped down the cherry tree?" Aaron joked as he eyed the fruit trees growing next to the path. Veronica shushed him. Willow was still counting.

"Forty-eight, forty-nine, fifty!" Willow stopped.

They stood at an intersection of the path, which now branched off in four different directions.

"North is left, Willow," Jasmine said. "Turn to the left and count out two hundred more steps. We're right behind you."

Willow turned and began her slow, steady counting as the others trailed behind. Jasmine felt her stomach flutter. They might be about to make the greatest discovery of their lives! Lili saw the look on her face and grabbed Jasmine's hand, giving it a little squeeze. They smiled at one another. This was it!

As Willow counted higher, they saw the path was leading them directly to a small red brick building with an old metal door.

"Gothic chic," Jasmine whispered to Lili, who smiled right back at her.

"One ninety-eight, one ninety-nine, two hundred!" Willow said triumphantly. She stood only a foot away from the front wall of the tiny structure.

"Is the treasure going to appear out of thin air now?" Aaron wondered, jokingly.

Willow consulted her visitor's guide. "It's called the Old Tomb. Washington wanted to be buried at Mount Vernon, but this tomb was deteriorating so he asked for a new one to be built. His body was moved to the new tomb after 1831, along with the remains of Martha and his other family members." Willow glanced up at the aged and weathered building. "So George and Martha were buried here before being moved to the new tomb, which I guess is why they call it the Old Tomb."

"That leaves us with the last clue from the sapphire," Lili said. "The Pythagorean or Masonic symbol, whatever you want to call it." She held up her hand. On it she had once again drawn the image found on the sapphire: three squares of different sizes, their corners touching so that the three linked sides of the squares formed a triangle. She shivered as she looked at the old building. "Will we have to go inside?"

Ryan shrugged. "Maybe. We'll have to figure out the final clue first."

Willow turned so that she was once again facing the red brick front of the Old Tomb. "Let's look around."

They all fanned out across the small front wall, looking intently at every nook and cranny in the brick surface.

"Nothing here." Ryan shook his head.

Aaron studied the old metal door with its rusty hinges. He threw his hands in the air. "Nothing on the door."

Veronica peered closer at a brick that was at about shoulder level. She squinted closely at it. "Guys! I think I found something!"

They hurriedly gathered around to peek over her shoulder. The brick she was staring at had a small, faded design carved into the upper right corner. It was the same symbol as on the sapphire!

Lili squealed and Jasmine felt her heart skip a beat.

Ryan reached out and gently touched the brick. It moved in the wall.

"It's loose!" Willow said. She looked around to make sure no other visitors were nearby. "Ryan, try and take it out."

Jasmine looked around nervously. "Some of us should shield him, in case somebody comes along."

Lili and Veronica quickly flanked Jasmine, blocking Ryan from anyone who might come down the path.

Ryan carefully pried the brick from the wall. It slid easily into his hands and he placed it on the ground. Willow and Aaron crowded around to peer into the hole. Willow used the flashlight app on her phone to illuminate the dark space. Another, older brick sat recessed in the wall. As the light beam travelled along it, they saw it had the same Masonic symbol as the outer brick had.

"Wow! I feel like I'm in a movie or something," Aaron said breathlessly.

Ryan grabbed the second brick and pulled it. Pieces broke off and crumbled as it came sliding out of the wall. He laid the second brick on the ground next to the first.

Willow aimed the light back into the hole. A mysterious bundle, wrapped carefully in decaying fabric, sat inside.

"I think we found it!" Willow cried.

Jasmine turned around to look. "What is it?"

"I'm not sure," Willow replied.

Willow and Ryan both started to reach their hands in at the same time.

Ryan quickly pulled his away. "Go for it, Willow," he said with a smile.

Willow reached inside and very gingerly pulled out the bundle. In the light of day, they could see the aged yellow fabric surrounding whatever was hidden inside. Overwhelmed by curiosity, Lili, Jasmine, and Veronica gathered around to look.

"Whatever it is, it's old," Veronica remarked.

Willow cautiously began to unwrap the fabric, some of it crumbling to dust in her hand when she touched it. As the fabric fell away, the rays of sun began to play on the item hidden inside, making it sparkle and glow.

The last piece of fabric fell off. They all gasped as they looked at the treasure cradled in Willow's hands. The smooth stone, the size of a golf ball, was like nothing Willow had ever seen before. It looked like it contained a glittering galaxy of swirling comets and stars in deep, beautiful colors: blue, red, purple, and green.

"Oh my gosh, it's a black opal!" Jasmine said excitedly. "I've never seen or heard of one this big."

"We did it!" Willow cried.

"Yes!" Ryan echoed.

Lili began jumping up and down in pure joy. Veronica beamed and grabbed Aaron in a huge hug. Everyone started laughing and cheering. They had found the treasure!

Aaron looked at the magnificent black opal, which seemed the opposite of its name as it dazzled in the sunlight. "Dude," he said to Ryan. "No wonder your uncle wanted this. It must be worth a fortune!"

A dark shadow descended over them, blocking out the sunlight.

"It is," Arthur said with an evil smile. "Hand it over."

Chapter Seventeen

Willow quickly put her hands behind her back.

"No," she said firmly. "This isn't Atkinson Prep. You're not the boss here."

Atkinson laughed. "You all seem to forget that you are children. Clever children, maybe, but still children."

"We're smarter than you," Ryan said angrily. "You wouldn't have anything if it weren't for us!"

"Again, you forget yourselves. I am the one who set you on this path to begin with," Atkinson smoothly argued. "I have known of the treasure for years . . . years! When I learned of the four jewels, I knew they must lead to something valuable beyond measure. And it looks as though I was right."

"This doesn't belong to any of us," Jasmine boldly argued. "It belongs to the Washingtons."

"You know what they say: finders, keepers . . ." Atkinson said, taking a step closer. "And I'm afraid I can't wait much longer. The salary of a school director is laughable, I'm afraid, and since my family insists on excluding me from the more profitable businesses, I must find additional streams of income."

"So you chose stealing? Nice," Jasmine said.

"It will be nice indeed, when I can stop babysitting a school full of snot-nosed brats and retire to the tropics," he said. "A black opal this size, and with this historical significance, could be worth millions."

"Too bad it's not yours," Ryan told him.

"That can easily be arranged," he said, charging toward Willow. "Give it to me!"

He was inches from Willow when she grinned and held up her hands — both empty. A look of anger and confusion crossed Atkinson's face. From the corner of his eye he saw Ryan sprinting away. Realizing that Willow must have handed the opal to him, he quickly lunged after his nephew, tackling him to the ground. Ryan pushed his uncle off and started to run again, but Atkinson grabbed his ankle, holding him down.

"Arthur Atkinson, you will stand down!"

Startled, Atkinson looked up toward the sound of the powerful female voice. A middle-aged woman marched up to him and pulled him off Ryan.

"Principal Frederickson!" Jasmine cried.

"Stay out of this!" Atkinson barked at the principal. "The boy has my treasure."

Ryan jumped up and brushed the dirt from his pants. Then he grinned and turned out his empty jeans pockets.

"Treasure? What treasure?" he asked.

Erin and Isabel came running up next, followed by Ms. Keatley and Mr. Haverford — and two burly security guards.

"Is everything all right here?" one of the guards asked.

"This man just attacked this young boy," Principal Frederickson said. "He needs to be escorted from the grounds, if not arrested."

"That is ridiculous!" Arthur Atkinson fumed. "That is my nephew, and he stole my treasure."

"I told you, I don't have any treasure," Ryan said. "Honestly, I don't know what he's talking about."

"You guys found the treasure?" Erin blurted out.

"What's all this about a treasure?" Ms. Keatley asked.

Principal Frederickson looked at Willow. "Is it true? Did you really find it?"

Jasmine stepped forward and held out her hand. The black opal glittered in the sunlight.

"It's true," she said.

Chapter Eighteen

"I'm very glad I decided to check up on you girls," Principal Frederickson said. "Things could have become very unfortunate for everyone."

A large group of people was gathered in the Martha Washington School library, where everything had started — the Jewels, Eli, the Rivals, Principal Frederickson, Ms. Keatley, Mr. Haverford, and the new acting director of Atkinson Preparatory School, Ryan's dad. After the chaotic events of the day before, they had agreed to meet and finally sort things out.

"I still don't understand," Erin said. "How did you show up at Mount Vernon at exactly the right time?"

"I never got over the feeling that you girls were still searching for the final jewel, and the treasure," she replied. "If I were your age, I would certainly find it hard to resist. Then when I saw your field trip scheduled, I thought you might be looking for clues again. I decided to go to Mount Vernon myself, and when I pulled into the parking lot, I saw Arthur Atkinson charging into the orientation center. By the time I caught up to him, he was assaulting poor Ryan."

"He didn't hurt me," Ryan said. "Anyway, I knew by running away I would distract him from whoever Willow had really given the treasure to."

"That was really smart," Willow said admiringly.

Principal Frederickson turned to Ms. Keatley. "And I would like to know why you and Mr. Haverford were not with the students."

Ms. Keatley looked a little uncomfortable. "Erin and Isabel got into a heated argument, and we tried to break it up. By the time we realized the others were gone we had lost them."

"Sorry about that," Erin said, a little sheepishly. "We knew we'd need something good to distract you with, and Isabel and I had gotten pretty good at arguing."

"Even though you always lose," Isabel said with a grin, and Erin smiled back.

"But remember, they found us again," Lili said. "All because of my awesome big brother."

Eli shrugged. "I never trusted Arthur Atkinson, so I got some of my Memento Mori friends to help me put a GPS on him. When I saw he was headed for Mount Vernon, I texted all the Jewels."

"As soon as I saw the text, I told Ms. Keatley and Mr. Haverford that the other kids were in trouble," Erin said. "Eli helped us find them because he'd pinpointed Atkinson's location. We grabbed the security guards on the way."

Ms. Keatley chimed in next. "So the whole time we've been 'immersion learning' you've really been looking for clues to a treasure?" She sounded a little hurt.

"Well, yes, but we learned a lot of stuff along the way, too," Erin said. "It helped us do better in quiz bowl, honest."

"It's still amazing to me that you guys actually found the treasure," said Mr. Haverford, holding up the Sunday newspaper. "You're famous!"

SIXTH GRADERS FIND LOST WASHINGTON TREASURE ON VERNON ESTATE, read the headline, with a picture of the black opal underneath.

Erin grinned. "Yeah, I'm glad those guards didn't believe Atkinson's story that the treasure was his."

"And I'm glad they bought *our* story that we saw that the brick was loose and the treasure dropped into our hands," Ryan added.

"I still can't believe we found such a huge black opal," Jasmine said. "No wonder Martha was keeping it hidden. They probably could have financed a whole army with it back then."

"Maybe, but I've been doing some research," Erin said. "There are some cool legends about black opals. One is that they mean bad luck for monarchs — like, for example, King George III of England. He was king during the Revolutionary War."

Veronica nodded. "I get it. So maybe it was, like, some kind of good luck charm for the Americans or something."

"Maybe we'll never know why they went to all that trouble to hide it," Lili said with a dreamy look in her eyes. "Maybe the real motive will always be a mystery."

"Whatever the reason, I'm so glad the opal will stay in Mount Vernon, where it belongs," said Jasmine. She gazed over at the empty case that once held the Martha Washington ruby. "It's too bad we don't know what Arthur Atkinson did with the other four jewels, though."

"But we do," said Ryan's dad, Charles Atkinson, a blonder and more distinguished-looking version of his brother Arthur.

He stood up and placed a black briefcase on the table in front of him. Then he opened the case to reveal four jewels on a field of black velvet: the Martha Washington ruby, the diamond, the emerald, and the Atkinson sapphire.

The room got quiet as everyone stared at the jewels, which gleamed beautifully against the black background.

"How did you get them?" Erin asked.

"As you know, there is not enough evidence to prosecute my brother," Mr. Atkinson answered. "But our family has removed him from his position at the school. And we convinced him to turn over the four jewels, in exchange for not cutting him out of the family completely. Fortunately, he hadn't sold them yet. He was waiting to make sure you kids were right about the treasure."

"So what will happen to them now?" Jasmine asked.

"The sapphire will remain at Atkinson, of course," he said. "And the emerald will be returned to its owner, Derrica Girard. Our family has decided to donate the diamond to the Metropolitan Museum of Art, where it was found. And the ruby is now back where it belongs."

He reached in the case, picked up the ruby necklace, and handed it to Principal Frederickson. The principal smiled, and gazed happily around at the assembled crowd. Just then she noticed the yearning look in Jasmine's eyes.

"Would you like to hold it before I put it back?" she asked.

"Yes, please," Jasmine said breathlessly.

Principal Frederickson gently placed it in Jasmine's open palm as her friends gathered around her. Jasmine had always admired the stone, sketching it countless times. She had only ever seen it underneath glass.

"It's so beautiful," she whispered.

"It is good to have it back here at the school," Principal Frederickson said. "But even so, I wish you girls had not put yourselves in danger like that. And I am sure your parents feel the same way."

The four Jewels exchanged glances. All of their parents had been called to the school once they got back from Mount Vernon, and they had tried to explain the events as best as they could. As a result, they were in varying degrees of trouble. Erin and Willow were both grounded from after-school activities for a week, and Lili's parents had nearly banned her from participating on the quiz bowl team. Jasmine's parents were curious, asking question after question. It almost seemed like Jasmine's mom wished she could have joined in the fun.

"Don't worry," Willow said. "Our days of tracking jewel thieves and chasing treasure are over. We've got more important things to worry about." She looked at her friends.

"Nationals!" they all cheered at once.

Chapter Nineteen

"We really should be studying for Nationals," Willow said a little worriedly as the Jewels walked the grounds of Mount Vernon a few days later.

"Willow, we've been studying nonstop for a week," Erin reminded her. "We need a break."

"Besides, we never got a really good look at the treasure," Jasmine added. "I am dying of curiosity!"

"It's amazing that Mount Vernon put it on display so fast," Lili remarked.

Willow nodded. "Everyone's been so curious about it, they decided to put it out to meet the demand," she said. "Then I read that they're going to send it on tour to museums around the country."

Jasmine shivered. "I still can't believe that we helped find it. It seems like a dream, doesn't it?"

Erin nodded. "It does. And what's even more unbelievable is that we're friends with the Rivals."

"No kidding," Lili agreed. "Did I hear you and Isabel making plans for a sleepover the other day?"

Erin gave a sheepish grin. "There's a twenty-four-hour Civil War marathon on the History Channel coming up," she said. "It's no fun watching those alone."

"It's no fun watching those *ever*," Lili teased.

Jasmine's mother, who had driven them to the museum, followed behind on the grass-lined path. She nodded toward a small brick building up ahead. "There's the museum, girls."

A line of people snaked outside the entrance to the Donald W. Reynolds Museum.

"Wow, the black opal is really popular," Jasmine remarked.

"Of course it is," Erin said. "It's an awesome discovery."

The line to see the treasure was a separate line from the museum entrance. Inside the museum, visitors could see personal items that belonged to the Washingtons, as well as paintings and sculptures. But today, everyone had come to see the black opal.

After a fifteen-minute wait, the girls and Mrs. Johnson finally reached the glass display case, where the black opal sat inside.

"It's even more amazing up close," Jasmine said, getting as near to the glass as she could. "I wish I had gotten a better look when I held it in my hand."

"It's like the more you look, the more colors you see," Lili said breathlessly. "I don't think I've ever seen anything so beautiful!"

"I still think it's so cool that Martha came up with all those clues and had them etched on the jewels," Jasmine remarked. "That was really smart."

"That's what I've been trying to tell you guys. She was a pretty awesome lady," Erin said.

"We should move on, girls," Jasmine's mom said. "There are a lot of people waiting behind us."

With a sigh, Jasmine broke away from the display, and all of the girls reluctantly left the opal behind. They headed to the food court, a lovely glass pavilion surrounded by a brick terrace with metal tables and chairs. They found an empty table and sat down next to a freshly green bush, where a yellow butterfly rested on top of the leaves.

"I saw online that they have a nice deli here," said Mrs. Johnson. "Who wants a sandwich?"

"Tuna, please," said Lili.

"Oh, make mine tuna, too," Willow said. "Fish is brain food, and my brain needs all the food it can get for tomorrow."

"I'll take a veggie sandwich, if they have one, Mom," Jasmine said.

Mrs. Johnson nodded. "What about you, Erin?"

"Ham, salami, cheese, turkey, tomato, lettuce, pickles, mayo, and mustard, please," Erin said. "On whole wheat."

Lili made a face. "That doesn't sound like brain food."

"Hey, I'm getting it on whole wheat," Erin protested. "That's healthy."

Willow sighed. "It probably doesn't matter what we eat. There are fifteen other teams competing in our category at Nationals, and one of them is the Rivals. We don't have a chance of winning the whole thing."

Jasmine frowned. "That doesn't sound like the Willow I know. You're our math expert. There's got to be some percentage of a chance, right?"

"Well, I haven't fully worked it out yet . . . but yes," Willow grudgingly admitted. "I just feel like we need to study more."

"Then we'll go to the library for another study session as soon as we get back," Jasmine said. She looked at Erin and Lili. "Right?"

Now it was Erin's turn to sigh, but she and Lili still gave the same answer.

"Right!" they said.

Willow smiled. "You know, no matter how we do tomorrow, we should be proud," she said. "We've had a great season."

"And we found Martha's treasure," Erin added. "I'd say it doesn't get much better than that."

"But we *will* win, and things will get even more awesome," Lili said confidently. She held out her right arm over the table.

"Arts and literature!" she cheered.

Erin put her right hand on top of Lili's. "History!"

"Science!" Jasmine said, adding her hand to the pile.

Willow put her hand on top of Jasmine's. "Math!"

Then the four girls cheered together.

"Gooooooooo Jewels!"

Chapter Twenty

"Eight to the third power is five hundred and twelve," Willow said.

"That is correct, and the Jewels are twenty points in the lead so there is no need for a follow-up question," announced the moderator. "The Jewels will be moving on to the next round."

Willow, Jasmine, Erin, and Lili walked across the stage and shook hands with the members of the opposing team. Then they ran offstage and erupted into squeals.

"We did it!" Willow cheered. "We're going into the finals!"

"I can't believe it," Jasmine said. "My hands are shaking."

Sixteen sixth-grade teams had started competing that morning. First, each team competed against one another. Then the winners of those eight matches competed in the second round. In the third round, the top four teams paired up to compete. Now there were only two teams left: the Jewels and the Rivals.

The kids from the New Jersey team they had just defeated approached them.

"Good match," said Zinnira, the team captain.

"Yeah, you guys know your stuff," said another member, Grace.

The girl next to her nodded. "I'm kind of relieved that you won," Nadia said. "Those Rivals are scary."

The last member of the team, Josemanuel, nodded. "Yeah, they're like robots."

"We used to feel that way, too," Erin said. "But they're pretty normal once you get to know them."

"We even beat them once," Jasmine said.

Zinnira looked impressed. "Nice. Well, good luck!"

"Thanks," Willow replied.

There was a short break before the final round, so the Jewels headed to the lounge backstage at the Kennedy Center Opera House, where the Nationals tournament was taking place. Ms. Keatley was waiting for them with a big smile on her face.

"I am so proud of you!" she said, hugging each of them. "You are tearing through this competition."

On the other side of the room, Mr. Haverford was in a huddle with the four Rivals. Ryan looked up when he saw the Jewels enter.

"Great job," he said. "I'm glad it's you guys we're going up against."

"Why? Because you think we're easy to beat?" Willow asked, suddenly feeling defensive.

"No way," Ryan said. "Because you're worthy competitors."

Willow's angry expression softened. "Thanks. You, too."

Aaron walked up to them. "You guys look nice," he said.

"Thanks," Willow said. "Lili came up with our outfits, like always."

Because Nationals was being held in the classic and rather fancy Kennedy Center Opera House, Lili had decided that their usual T-shirts just wouldn't cut it. Instead, they each wore a ruby-red blouse with a black skirt and shoes.

"They are much better than those glittery shirts you wear," Isabel remarked.

"We've still got glitter," Erin said, pointing to the sparkling pin on her collar. "Lili made one for each of us in honor of the four jewels. Mine's blue, like the sapphire, see? Jasmine's looks like rubies, Willow's is diamonds, and Lili's got a green emerald."

Veronica stepped up and got a closer look at Erin's pin. Lili had created a swirly design using blue glass jewels.

"Wow, that's cool," she said admiringly.

"I can make some for you, too!" Lili said. "After all, we found the jewels together."

"That would be nice," Veronica agreed.

Lili turned to the boys. "Don't worry. I'll make you some cufflinks or something."

A young woman wearing a headset walked into the lounge. "You guys are back onstage in five minutes," she said.

Jasmine's palms immediately began to sweat. "Oh my gosh! I can't believe we're in the finals!"

Ryan held out his hand to Willow. "May the best team win!"

The Jewels and Rivals solemnly shook hands with one another, and then headed back onstage.

Ever after a full day of competing there, the opera house still felt like the most magnificent stage they'd ever been on. The hall was huge, with three levels of balconies. The seats and balcony facades were a rich red velvet.

"It's like being inside a ruby," Jasmine whispered as they walked back to their microphones.

"I just realized that, too," Erin whispered back. "Maybe that's good luck!"

The quiz bowl moderator was already standing at the lectern. There was a different moderator for this round, and this time a woman with short gray hair and glasses had the job.

"Welcome to the last round of the Grade Six National Quiz Bowl

Championship," she announced. "Competing today are the Atkinson Preparatory Rivals and the Martha Washington Jewels, both from the Washington, DC, area."

A cheer went up from the crowd. It was hard to see faces because of the bright lights on stage, but Willow shaded her eyes to make sure Principal Frederickson, Ms. Keatley, and all their parents were still there. Seeing her mom's face always made her feel a little bit calmer.

"The rules are the same as the previous rounds," the moderator went on. "The first team to buzz in after a question has the opportunity to answer. If the answer is correct, they will be asked three follow-up questions. If the answer is incorrect, the other team will have a chance to respond."

Willow tightened her hand around her buzzer, and looked down the row at her teammates. Jasmine, Erin, and Lili were all doing the same. They were ready to go.

"First question," the moderator began. "A book is on sale for fifteen dollars. If the sale price is twenty-five percent off the original cost, what was the original price?"

Another math question, Willow thought, and she quickly did the calculations in her head. She buzzed in — one second later than Ryan.

"Twenty dollars," Ryan replied.

"Correct," the moderator said, and Willow felt her stomach flip. Was this how the rest of the match was going to go?

The Rivals got three follow-up math questions right, and with each question worth ten points, they were leading the Jewels 40–0 right out of the gate. Willow gripped the buzzer even more tightly.

"What is the scientific name that describes rocks that have melted and then cooled and solidified?" the moderator asked.

Jasmine hit the buzzer so quickly that Willow nearly jumped out of her skin.

"Igneous!" she practically shouted when the moderator called on her.

"Correct," she said. "And now for your follow-up questions."

The next three questions were also about geology, Jasmine's specialty, and the score was now tied at 40–40.

The next question was about the Little House on the Prairie books, and Aaron got to it before Lili could buzz in. Willow was starting to feel a sense of déjà vu. Every time they faced the Rivals, it was like a tennis match. The Rivals got one right, and then the Jewels got one right. If the Rivals missed a follow-up question, the Jewels missed one on their next turn.

It's going to be right down to the last question, Willow thought. She could feel it. With the Rivals, there was always going to be suspense.

And Willow was right.

"This is the last toss-up question," the moderator said as the match drew to a close. "The Jewels and Rivals are tied, so if one team gives the correct answer to this question they will win the match — and the Grade Six National Quiz Bowl Championship."

A hush went over the crowd as the moderator picked up the last card — the card that would decide everything.

"Name the lawyer who wrote the lyrics to the United States' national anthem, 'The Star-Spangled Banner,'" the moderator said.

Erin and Isabel buzzed in at what sounded like almost exactly the same time. The moderator looked to one of the judges offstage, who walked on and conferred with her. Willow's heart was beating like a drum.

"Martha Washington gets the question," the moderator said, and Willow let out a huge sigh of relief.

Erin grinned. "That would be Francis Scott Key."

"Correct," the moderator said. "Congratulations, Jewels. You are the Grade Six National Quiz Bowl Champions!"

This time, the girls couldn't hold back their cheering. They jumped up and down, hugging one another. A man in a suit walked onstage with a three-foot-tall trophy that he placed in Willow's arms.

The Rivals walked over to them.

"I can't say I'm happy we lost," Veronica said. "But at least you guys won."

"Thanks!" Willow said. "It was hard beating you guys."

"Yeah, it came right down to the wire there," Erin said, looking at Isabel.

"It was *too* close," Isabel said with a grin. "We will beat you next time."

Both teams posed for photos for their excited parents before heading backstage to gather their things and leave. Willow placed the trophy on a table and everyone gathered around to admire it.

"It's so shiny," Lili said, touching the silver cup.

"I like the design of the plaque," Jasmine said, pointing to a black plate engraved with symbols for science, math, history, and the arts. Then Jasmine frowned. "Wait, there's something sticking out from behind the plaque."

Jasmine tugged at a piece of yellow paper tucked behind the engraved plate and pulled out a small, folded note. She opened it up to reveal a message that looked like it had been typed on an old typewriter.

The four lost jewels have all been found,
But many treasures still abound.

Willow looked at Ryan. "Very cute. When did you plant this?"

Ryan shook his head. "I didn't." And Willow started smiling in disbelief.

"I swear, I didn't!" he insisted

"Of course you did," Jasmine said. "It's on the same lined paper as those notes you sent us before."

"But the writing is different," Erin pointed out, and silence descended on the group.

Lili's eyes were wide. "Well, if Ryan didn't send it, then who did?" she asked.

The Jewels and Rivals looked at one another questioningly, but no one had an answer.

"Don't tell me we have more jewels to find," Jasmine said, but her voice sounded more hopeful than complaining.

Erin put a finger to her lips. "Shhh, don't let Principal Frederickson hear you say that," she said, and everyone laughed.

"Seriously, guys, what if we get another message?" Lili asked.

"Then we'll do what we do best, and try to figure it out," Willow said. "After all, we're the Jewels!"

"*And* the Rivals!" Ryan chimed in. All eight teammates looked at one another and grinned. They would do it together!

The End

SNIFF OUT MYSTERIES, DIG UP CLUES,

Collar the CULPRIT...

a DOG and his GIRL MYSTERIES

Play DEAD

Jane B. Mason and Sarah Hines Stephens

SCHOLASTIC

...DON'T MISS

a DOG and his GIRL MYSTERIES